The Hostage

by

Jonas Saul

PUBLISHED BY:

Imagine Press Inc.
Ebook ISBN: 978-1-927404-05-8
Paperback ISBN: 978-1-927404-81-2
Hardcover ISBN: 978-1-998047-21-5

The Hostage

The Sarah Roberts Series

Dark Visions (One)
The Warning (Two)
The Crypt (Three)
The Hostage (Four)
The Victim (Five)
The Enigma (Six)
The Vigilante (Seven)
The Rogue (Eight)
Killing Sarah (Nine)
The Antagonist (Ten)
The Redeemed (Eleven)
The Haunted (Twelve)
The Unlucky (Thirteen)
The Abandoned (Fourteen)
The Cartel (Fifteen)
Losing Sarah (Sixteen)
The Pact (Seventeen)
The Terror (Eighteen)
The Chase (Nineteen)
The Betrayal (Twenty)
Sarah's Return (Twenty-One)
The Hunt (Twenty-Two)
The Delivery (Twenty-Three)
The Trap (Twenty-Four)
The Ultimatum (Twenty-Five)
The Depraved (Twenty-Six)
The Condemned (Twenty-Seven)
Payback (Twenty-Eight)
The Unknown (Twenty-Nine)
Wrath (Thirty)
The Damned (Thirty-One)
The Game (Thirty-Two)

The Decoy (Thirty-Three)
The Disappearance (Thirty-Four)
The Whole Truth (Thirty-Five)
Alex (Thirty-Six)
Parkman (Thirty-Seven)
Darwin (Thirty-Eight)
Aaron (Thirty-Nine)
Remains To Be Seen (Forty)

The Jake Wood Novels

The Immortal Gene (Book One)
The Immortal Target (Book Two)

Standalone Novels

'Til Death Do Us Part
The Drowning
The Woman in the Woods
The Threat
The Specter
The Mafia Trilogy
A Murder in Time
Frequency of the Dead

Co-Authored Novels

Collision Course (Written with Gary Ponzo)
There Will Be Blood (Written with Rania Stone)
The Soulless (Written with Rania Stone)

Short Story Collections

Twisted Fate (Tales of Horror)

Twists of Fate (Tales of Hope)

5

Twists of Fate (Tales of Hope)

Chapter 1

Sᴀʀᴀʜ Rᴏʙᴇʀᴛꜱ ᴡᴏɴᴅᴇʀᴇᴅ ɪꜰ intent mattered. Could murder be justified?

She rested her head back on the seat and contemplated what her life had become—debating the senseless murder of Drake Bellamy and thinking about her dead sister. What caused Vivian to stay in touch?

After she stopped Drake's planned murder, would she be able to find out why Drake was targeted? All the key players were already dead. There had to be a reason other than just murder.

Turbulence snapped Sarah out of her thoughts as the Boeing 747-400 shook. They dropped through the clouds as she rubbed her stomach. The plane's in-flight meal hadn't sat well.

The ground took shape below, Toronto sprawling to all points on the compass except where Lake Ontario touched its southern shore.

The lake had the look of an ocean due to its massive size.

From where she sat, a few thousand feet in the air, the lake stopped at the horizon. The United States couldn't be seen on the other side.

The lone male passenger beside her had slept most of the flight but was waking now. She had the window seat in a row of three. An empty chair separated the man who had introduced himself as Dave when they'd first sat down. Heading home to a funeral, he'd said. How sad.

A commotion started in front of her seat. The couple in the next row were arguing. She looked at Dave and smiled at the tension in the seats ahead. Then she heard the woman gasp. Sarah looked out the window again but only saw the sprawling city and the massive lake. She'd never been to Toronto, but she'd seen pictures, so she had an idea of what to expect. She scanned the downtown area, but for all her effort, she couldn't locate the CN Tower, one of Toronto's landmark tourist attractions.

Something's wrong. That's why they're arguing.

Her stomach dropped.

What now?

She looked at the man beside her again. He seemed disinterested in the people ahead of them as they grew more and more animated.

A beep resounded throughout the aircraft, signaling everyone to fasten their seat belts. Sarah already had hers on. She looked out the window again as they got closer to the ground.

"This is your captain speaking. Good afternoon. We'll be landing in Toronto to moderate winds, with a light cloud cover and a temperature of twenty-eight degrees Celsius. We're slightly ahead of schedule as we had a tailwind. We'll be landing fifteen minutes early. The cabin crew and I would like to thank you for flying KLM flight 487B and wish you safe travels wherever your final destination may be. Cabin crew, take your seats for landing."

Sarah stared out the window as the city drew closer. No CN Tower. Nothing recognizable. Weird.

Toronto's big. Maybe it's in another area.

The couple in the seats in front of her grew louder. The man pushed the flight attendant button.

Sarah tapped the back of their seat and leaned forward.

"Is everything okay?" she asked. "Now that we're preparing to land, I don't think any flight attendants will come."

Both of them turned and looked at her through the gap in the seat.

"That's not Toronto below us," the male said. "Something's wrong. We're landing in Chicago. That body of water down there is Lake Michigan, not Lake Ontario."

"What?" Sarah was stunned. They had to be making a mistake. "Are you sure? The captain just announced that we were landing in Toronto."

"I'm absolutely sure. I used to live there. This is Chicago. No doubt about it."

"But why? There's no layover booked there. Let me check my boarding pass."

Sarah reached into her carry-on bag and grabbed her boarding pass, already knowing she wouldn't see the name Chicago on it. It said KLM, flight 487B, her seat number, and the destination: Toronto. She had to be in Toronto by Wednesday to stop Drake Bellamy's murder. If she was on the wrong flight, she had no idea how long it would take to make new plans.

"What do your boarding passes say?" she asked.

"They say we're on a flight to Toronto. It doesn't make any sense because that's Chicago below us."

Sarah turned to her right. Dave, the man sitting one seat over, had a stupid smile on his face.

"Have you checked your boarding pass?"

He shook his head in the negative but didn't say anything more.

"Why are you smiling?" Sarah frowned. "What's so amusing?"

Dave opened the right side of his jacket far enough to show Sarah a weapon.

"I'm an air marshal. The penalties and jail time can be severe for air rage, so I suggest you sit back and relax. Don't do anything stupid. No more disturbing the other passengers, either. No more questions. There's nowhere you can go, nothing you can do. Stay calm. Everything will be explained when we land."

Sarah stared at him, open-mouthed. "Tell me you're joking, please, because showing me that"—she pointed at his gun—"I consider it a threat. I've done nothing wrong on this flight. I've not been arrested, and I'm definitely not your prisoner. So, tell me you're joking, because if you aren't, we are going to have a problem. A serious fucking problem."

The air marshal undid his seat belt and stood up in the aisle. He looked toward the back of the plane and nodded once. He turned forward and repeated the same nod.

Two men walked toward Dave along the aisle.

Dave turned to the passengers watching him from their seats when his backup arrived.

"May I have your attention, please? My name is Dave Ingram. I am an air marshal. These men are also marshals. We have a temporary situation that you needn't be alarmed with. This plane is landing in Chicago, and then it will be heading to Toronto as planned. You may be a little late getting to your final destination, and we're sorry for that inconvenience, but we have a passenger here that needs to be detained. Stay calm. We'll be on the ground in moments."

What a nightmare. Who was orchestrating this?

People whispered among themselves. Sarah felt every face aimed toward her. She needed to think. They were close to the ground. The plane would touch down within a minute. She had to do something, but what?

Could Rod Howley be behind this? No way. He's dead or seriously wounded back in Hungary.

She leaned her head back and closed her eyes as the wheels touched down.

Stay calm, Sarah, stay calm.

There was no use trying to fight three armed men. With the way air travel had changed, regular passengers would come to their aid if she attacked the marshals.

What will Parkman think when he arrives in Toronto to pick her up at the airport and, not only is flight 487B late, but Sarah isn't on it? He is going to be pissed. They were supposed to meet and go to a ball game tomorrow to see the stadium before Wednesday, the day Drake is to be killed. Parkman will be furious when he finds out who's behind this.

I'm going to be furious when I find out who has fucked up my day.

The air brakes activated, and the plane slowed, taxiing off the landing strip.

The three marshals wouldn't take their eyes off of her. Whoever was behind this had informed these men who she was and that she was to be watched carefully. Do not underestimate her. Sarah is dangerous.

Good advice.

Sarah undid her belt. The plane stopped, still quite far from the terminal. In the distance, a line of three black SUVs headed their way.

FBI?

The couple sitting ahead of her sneaked peeks backward. She smiled at the woman, who jumped away as if bitten.

"Is all this really necessary?" Sarah asked.

Dave nodded.

"Who has the kind of power to change the flight plan of a major commercial airliner?" Sarah asked. "The U.S. government, maybe? The Sophia Project guys? Am I getting closer?"

Dave didn't respond this time. He bent down and looked out Sarah's window at the approaching SUVs.

"They're coming now," he said to the two men on either side of him.

Obviously, she wasn't going to get anything out of Dave before whoever was coming got there. She crossed her arms, laid back, and closed her eyes. This didn't bother her. She wouldn't allow it to. Whoever was behind it, whatever they wanted, she would fix it and move on. That was the way of things for her. It had always been that way and always will be.

"Where are your bags?" Dave asked.

"I don't have any bags," she said, keeping her eyes closed. "Only this carryon by my feet. I travel light."

The door to the plane opened. She sat eight rows back from where she had boarded. Boots smacked down hard as several people entered the aircraft in unison. She opened her eyes and looked up, hoping to recognize someone who could answer her questions.

A line of military-type recruits in green camouflage stomped down the aisle toward Dave and his men, who moved away to give the newcomers more room. Within seconds, Sarah's seat was surrounded by eight beefy men.

The tallest one stepped in close and asked in a deep John Wayne voice, "Are you, Sarah Roberts?"

"Who's asking?"

"Stand up," he ordered. "Now."

"Fuck you. First, tell me what this is all about. I bought a ticket to fly to Toronto. I'm an American citizen. I cannot be held without being charged and since I've done nothing wrong, tell me what this is all about."

"Sarah Roberts, you are under arrest for the murder of Joseph Singer. Stand up, or my men will drag you out. Your choice will either be hard or easy, but we prefer hard."

It felt like someone smacked her in the face. She had never heard the name Joseph Singer before. There had to be a mistake. Where did this kind of shit come from? Could life ever be normal, or did it always have to be fucked? And how could they re-route a plane just to arrest one person? Wouldn't they get the Canadian authorities to pick her up as she exited the plane in Toronto and then extradite her through the normal legal process?

Someone set this up. Someone is setting me up.

All eyes in the immediate area were on her. She was sure the passengers surrounding her seat weren't thinking about their delay to Toronto anymore. They wanted to see some action.

Fucking rubberneckers.

"Hard or easy, huh?" she asked. "Those are my options?"

"Wait!" a man yelled from down the aisle near the front of the plane. Heads turned to see the new arrival. A man in a long black overcoat and a black fedora made his way toward her.

Rod Howley. *Motherfucker*.

"Ahh," Sarah said. "Now I understand what's happening here."

"Fall back, men. Give her a chance to stand on her own legs before they're both broken."

"Is that how it's going to be?" Sarah asked. "How did you do it? How could you reroute this plane? Are you that powerful now?"

The thin aisle offered little wiggle room when two well-built men needed to pass one another. Rod forced his way through as best he could and stopped at her seat.

"Sarah, we have danced together too long. It's over. You're on American soil now. You're mine. You don't have Parkman here to help. No one on this plane knows who you are." He leaned closer. "Have you no honor? Do this to help your fellow American. Have you no soul? Do what I need you to do to help your fellow human being. Come with me willingly and show me what you're made of. Help me help them," he said, waving an arm around the cabin.

She looked away. Outside, she saw a distant city, grass, and tarmac. It looked like the terminal stood a mile away. Even if she figured out how to get past this many men, where would she run to?

He had finally done it. He got her. She had no choice.

Without looking at him, she said, "Yes, I have a soul. That's why I do what I do in the first place. That's why I fight for the weak and won't work for the government."

The couple in the seat in front of her gasped simultaneously. She realized they were assuming she justified murder in such a way.

It was time to leave. This wasn't the place or the time to make a stand.

"I'll come peacefully," she said. "Step back, give me some room, and I will leave this plane with you."

"You're right. You'll be leaving this plane with me."

"Cocky much?" Sarah asked.

Rod stepped back and motioned for his men to give her room. Sarah lifted her carry-on and edged along the seats until she reached the aisle, where she stood and turned to face Rod.

"You bastard. You, sir, are a fucking whore. You have sold your soul to the government. I think I will have to kill you one day, Rod Howley. There will come a time when I will fear you no more."

Rod didn't smile. He didn't act cocky. He stepped aside and nodded.

Sarah's legs were swept out from under her. She barely had enough time to brace herself and protect her face as she hit the carpeted floor of the airplane aisle. She tried to spin onto her back but couldn't. Too many men pounced at the same time. Someone's knee jammed into her back with another knee on her neck. They were doing something to her feet.

It ended as fast as it started. Rough hands grabbed her

and lifted until she stood on her feet again. She looked down at the two large, iron cuffs on her ankles, connected by a chain.

"Are you serious?"

A nearby passenger asked Rod if that was necessary. Rod cautioned him to mind his own business.

"You will not run from me again," Rod said. "I assure you of that."

Her carry-on bag lay on the aisle floor, having slipped off her shoulder when she was knocked down. One of the men grabbed it.

"Hey!"

Another man grabbed her forearm and, before she could stop him, slapped handcuffs on her wrists. He stepped behind her and turned her shoulders until she faced Rod again.

"There. You're all tied up and ready for transport to prison. Let's go."

Rod turned and started up the aisle. Sarah caught a glimpse of the couple who had sat in front of her. The woman shook her head back and forth in disgust.

If they only knew.

Sarah shuffled forward as the ankle cuffs offered little leeway. A staircase had been rolled up to the side of the plane. The sun broke through the clouds, reflecting off the white metal steps. The space between her ankles wasn't enough to manage the stairs. Even before she could protest, a man on either side lifted an arm each and carried her down the steps to the tarmac, where they set her back down.

Both her arms felt like they'd be bruised badly. All the way down, she fought the urge to scream from the pain of their combined grip.

The SUVs all sat with their doors open. They guided her to the middle one parked near the tip of the airplane's wing.

Rod moved up beside her. No one spoke. She knew the drill. Do this, do that, comply with them, and then find a hole in Rod's armor. She'd get out. There's a way. There was always a way.

At the vehicle, the ankle cuffs prevented her from lifting her leg high enough to enter, so she turned to Rod.

He grabbed her hair behind her right ear and twisted her head back until his face loomed over hers.

"Shit, that hurts," she said through clenched teeth.

Water filled her eyes. It had been a while since that much hair had been pulled at the same time.

"You're mine now," Rod said, his nose an inch from hers. "We parlayed too much in Europe. Until I'm satisfied you have a gift or not, you will never be out of my sight again. Got it?"

She tried to nod. When he let go, she righted her head, the pain fresh and sharp.

The man behind her held a baton.

Where the fuck did that come from?

He lifted it and swung.

She had no chance.

The end of the baton hit her in the exact spot where Rod had pulled on her hair.

Sarah was out before she hit the tarmac.

Chapter 2

ELMORE ACKERMAN LOOKED OUT his kitchen window as he poured his coffee. He thought about his prisoner in the basement and how sweet she was. Had he broken Jackie yet? Was it time for a new slave? Maybe she needed further lessons, one that brought out the animal side of human nature. Or maybe she just needed to die quickly so he could move on.

He set the pot back, stirred and sipped his coffee, and then started for his office. Jackie could wait in her cage. He would deal with her later tonight or tomorrow. By then, he would have decided her fate.

He turned on his MacBook at his desk and brought up his finance page for the twenty-two vending machines he had scattered across Japan. The used panty business had been flourishing for years. Japan was the leading country selling used panties, and Elmore was no stranger to the business. Vending machines had popped up all over Japan, with Elmore's machines going in almost two years ago. Now it financed all of his ventures, from the cages in the basement to his photo studio in downtown Toronto where he collected the best panty shots for verification and authenticity.

Craigslist had made him a certain amount over the years, but the vending machines were his golden goose.

He leaned on the desk with his elbow while he picked at the ten-year-old scab on the side of his head. He'd banged his head many years ago, and it had never healed properly. He wouldn't leave the scab alone, picking it until it bled. Only recently had he tried to calm it down to facilitate healing, but the Jackie situation stressed him out. She'd been his sex partner for almost six months now. He had grown bored recently. He needed someone new. And Jackie cried through the night too much for his liking.

A piece of the scab came off and lodged under his nail. He examined his nail and then eased the small piece of bloody crust out from under it, tossing it in the trash can.

Elmore opened the desk drawer on his right and grabbed a little black container that originally held a roll of film. He flipped off the lid and looked inside. The fingernails stored within were for moments like this. A few of his were there, along with Jackie's and the girls who came before her. He shuffled the contents and grabbed one of the thicker toenails. Then, carefully, he placed the lid back on the film container and set it on his desk.

After another sip of his coffee, Elmore eased the toenail between his front teeth and began the long task of diligently rolling the nail between all of his teeth over and over. He could never get bored with a good nail in his mouth. The simple pleasure of moving the nail around the tongue and between the teeth brought back wonderful memories of dead girls buried on his property. Girls who had performed beyond their years and given him hundreds upon hundreds of photos for his panty business at no charge. Actually, they paid him with their feminine gifts.

He examined the sales increases on his computer screen and smiled, the nail stuck near his molars. He scratched another piece of the scab off his head, tossing it in the trash after careful examination.

The sun shone through the window behind him, bright and warm on his back. At that moment, he decided: Jackie needed to go. He would get a new girl this week; he was sure of it. The scab on his head felt great. Sales were up. Life was good, and Elmore needed to kill again. The urge was too intense to ignore.

Maybe one day he could get the girl he had always dreamed of. Women like Jackie were kind and gentle. Elmore felt he needed a challenge. Girls like Sarah Roberts, now that would be fun. He wondered how she'd react to being photographed in a pair of panties. He wondered how she'd take the drugged sex and violence he enjoyed.

On the opposite wall sat a large cork board that Elmore had purchased at a store that catered to teachers. Every picture he could ever find of Sarah Roberts sat on the cork board. The newspapers had reported on her exploits at a Mormon compound. Elmore had been able to locate old editorials on people Sarah had saved from kidnappings, burning buildings, and car accidents. It was amazing and awe-inspiring. Not many women had those kinds of talents and those kinds of looks. Sarah Roberts was model-stunning gorgeous. There was no doubt about it.

"One day, Sarah Roberts," Elmore said, staring at the

pictures across the room on his wall. "I will get you, and the two of us will have many months to get to know each other better. I'm sure you taste as good as you look."

He lifted his coffee, toasted her, and took a large sip. Before he could stop it, the coffee washed the toenail down his throat as he swallowed.

"Shit."

He grabbed the black container, pulled out another long, thick one, placed it near his wisdom teeth, and shoved it down in between. His tongue found the nail and began to coax it around.

He had studied Sarah ever since she was rumored to have saved a news anchorwoman from a car accident on the St. Elizabeth Bridge almost five years ago. She had recently been to Hungary, and she would want to come back to North America soon.

"Knowledge is power, and Elmore is knowledge," he said to the empty room.

Sarah was everything he desired. The only small problem he felt he could get over was her age. She was at least seven years older than he would normally look for in a hostage. At twenty-four, she had been used up too much, but Elmore was willing to let that go, if only for a year of her time. One year in the cage, her food drugged and blacked out most of the time, she'd become dependent on him and learn to love him. Then, when completely docile, she would bore him, and he'd give her a proper burial out back. She deserved it after all the people she'd saved. If only he could tell where she'd be next.

"Where will you turn up next, Sarah?" he asked out loud.

A few of the newspapers he'd read suggested that Sarah had died in the Danube River outside Esztergom, Hungary, but he knew that to be false. Sarah was too tough, too strong. She'd turn up again, and he would be waiting when she did.

Elmore picked up the black container and spit the nail back in. He replaced the container on his desk and stood.

"Sorry, Jackie, but you have to go. Sarah's coming. I'm sure of it, and I want to be ready. Gotta make room for her. She's on her way, and wherever she lands, I will find a way there and find her. Then I will bring her back here. I will own Sarah Roberts. She will be my little pet."

Elmore walked away from his desk and headed for the basement, a crooked smile on his face. Maybe he should have Jackie one more time before he killed her. Or, maybe one more time after he killed her. He'd decide when she showed him how much she loved him.

He opened the basement door and started down the stairs, becoming aroused with each step.

Chapter 3

THE PAIN NEVER SEEMED to stop. Sarah woke slowly, sprawled out on the hard floor of a small, dank room. Any sort of movement caused her headache to flare. It felt like a brain-eating cockroach working on her insides, and the little light in the room caused it to scurry through her frontal lobe, searching for a hiding spot but finding none.

With both hands on her temples, massaging in slow circles, Sarah tried to roll over and get to her feet, but she did this act of bravery as slowly as her fingers moved.

A single bulb hung suspended from the ceiling, lighting what looked like an interrogation room. She had been in many over her short life. This one was no different other than the wet, musty smell.

A wooden table and chair sat to her right. She crawled over and got on the chair with great effort. She eased her head down to the table and rested it, forehead to wood until the pain rescinded.

Her right hand felt around the back of her head and then

her neck, pushing the muscles in that area to loosen them up. Something flicked across her fingers. She shouted out in pain.

"What the fuck?"

She touched the back of her neck again, this time more careful to not push or cause further damage. Stitches were sewn into her skin behind her ear, just under the hairline.

Did that guy hit me with the baton so hard it split my skin? No wonder I'm in so much pain.

She raised her head high enough to look at the two-way glass.

"Assholes, get me some fucking Advil. And get me Rod Howley. Tell him I want to talk. But not until I have a conversation with Mr. Advil. We have business to attend to first."

She lowered her head slowly and rested it on the wooden table, her fingers at work on her temples again.

She wondered why Vivian hadn't warned her about Rod. Or maybe told her to take a different flight. Was this one of those, let Sarah walk into a trap, only to break her out and, in doing so, catch the bad guys as that was the only way to nail them? If that's the way it's supposed to be, that sucked. She hated having to figure shit out as it happened. People got hurt that way. Sarah got hurt that way.

Rod was powerful. His government gave him more control over others than he should have. They had an agenda, and it was to be achieved at all costs. She wondered what their real agenda was and why the urgency. If they really believed Sarah had some kind of psychic powers, which evidently they did, then Rod had shown her he could do anything to detain her. If she was really psychic, couldn't she have seen him coming? Would she ever get out, or were they that powerful? Could Rod and his group make her disappear?

She understood that her situation grew increasingly dire each and every day. The longer she stayed locked up, her chances of escape worsened. But if she showed them what they wanted, Sarah felt she'd never get out. Their appetite would never be sated.

The door to the room cracked open, and something got tossed in. She looked down at a small bottle of Advil as it settled a few feet from her chair. Moving her head ever so slowly, she scanned more of the floor but couldn't find any water.

Fuck it. I'll chew the little bastards.

She lowered herself off the chair and slumped to the floor. The pain stayed constant but didn't spike as she took care to move slowly and calculated. The Advil bottle held six tablets. She popped all six in her mouth, chewed and swallowed them as fast as she could, then lay back and stared at the ceiling.

Ten minutes, maybe fifteen, and I'll feel this knife lift out of my skull.

The door opened again. Someone stepped in and closed it behind them. Sarah didn't bother to look. Whoever it was would present themselves soon enough. Her visitor walked the few steps to the table and slammed something on the top hard enough to flare her head.

"Fucking asshole. I asked for Advil because I have a headache the size of Texas. Don't slam things around, or I'll get pissed off. Right now, I'd prefer to not have any fun, so stay quiet."

"I'm afraid I can't stay quiet," Rod Howley said. "We

have business."

She opened her eyes and toward him. "We don't have any business. Unless that business is you opening that door over there and escorting me outside to wave goodbye with that funny hat you wear on your head. By the way, how long have I been here? What day is it?"

She closed her eyes again and heard him walk closer. When she opened them, his face took the place of a ceiling tile. It really bothered her to see him every time she turned around in Europe, and now here he was again. She had tried to evade him. Almost died in the Danube, only to be pulled out by Parkman. They had been flown by helicopter to Romania and escorted to a private airport after most of her wounds had healed. Parkman had taken an earlier flight and was supposed to be in Toronto waiting for her. Rod had somehow seen through all that, and here he was again.

He nudged her with his foot. "Get up. It's Wednesday morning. You've been here for two days. Now, get up, I have pictures to show you."

Two days? Wednesday? Drake is going to be shot Wednesday afternoon. Could there still be time?

"You talk first. Let the Advil get a grip on my headache. Hey, by the way, why the hell did your guy have to hit me hard enough to cause stitches? What was that for? I was handcuffed and shackled, for fuck sake."

"Yeah, sorry about that. That was excessive. I ordered everyone to think of you as an enemy combatant who had infiltrated our rank to kill all of us. By the time we had you cuffed, my men were pretty pissed at you. I didn't think it would go that far."

"Thanks, dick fuck. Now I've got a nice-sized migraine,

and you're still a dick. Help me up, and we'll walk out of here together and forget this whole misunderstanding."

Sarah raised both her arms and waited.

"Forget it, Sarah. I won't be touching you. I'm still healing from Hungary, too. I won't risk my life tangling with you right now. Get up on your own, or I'll have the men standing behind that mirror come in and put you in that chair. You don't want that, so get up."

Sarah lowered her arms and rolled onto her side. Doing her best to avoid any sudden movements, she got up and sat in the chair. The pain in her head showed signs of receding already.

Oh Advil, blessed Advil, oh how I love thee.

"Sarah, I need you to show me how you do your automatic writing. Work with me, and I will make your stay with us much more comfortable than this. Trust me. The ones who comply get whatever they want. Your life would be so much better and less dangerous than it currently is."

Sarah raised a hand for him to stop. "What are you talking about? What's automatic writing?"

"Don't bullshit me, Sarah. Before I came to Europe, I talked to Esmerelda, Dolan, and many others. I know what you are and how accurate you can be. Your talents have to be clinically tested. We have to show it working and have proof."

"You lie," Sarah said, her head clearing even more. She blinked slowly and then watched Rod for every facial movement, every nuance, in an attempt to figure out what he was up to.

"About what?"

"There's no way Esmerelda or Dolan would have

betrayed my confidence. They would have never talked freely with someone like you. Not about me, anyway."

"Ahh, but they did," Rod said, holding up his right index finger. "What they didn't know was who I am. They thought I was a writer who had been saved from that burning building a few years back. They thought I already knew about your abilities. Neither one thought what they told me was news to me."

"Let me get this straight. You just knocked on their door and chatted about me? That's it? Is that how it happened?"

"Not exactly. I posed as a cab driver for Dolan. We chatted for an hour in New York traffic. I told him that you and I talked once in a while and that I missed you. Esmerelda and I talked it up when a bouquet of flowers were mistakenly sent to her home address. I delivered the flowers and told her I recognized her name. Wasn't she the friend of Sarah Roberts, who was also my friend? Boy, can that woman talk. She was so appreciative of what you did for her daughter."

Sarah stared at him. If she had a weapon of any kind at that moment, she would have used it and screw the consequences. Rod had gone too far.

"I refuse to be your guinea pig."

"Look, Sarah, you tracked Armond Stuart around the world with no resources but your own wits and your sister, Vivian. Do you expect me to believe you're just lucky? That you're an average twenty-four-year-old girl? How do you manage a task like that without help? Some of our best FBI agents can't do what you've done. Give me something to go on."

Sarah moved her head back and forth slowly.

"What?" Rod asked. "What's that? Your answer?"

"I want a glass of water."

Rod raised his right hand and snapped his fingers. They waited, looking at each other. The door opened, and a man walked in, set a bottle of water on the table, and promptly left the room.

Sarah opened the bottle, drank half of it, and addressed Rod.

"You can't hold me," Sarah said. "Maybe your government gives you extra powers, but twenty-four hours tops, and I'll be out of here. Save your bullshit for someone else."

Rod shook his head. "I'm afraid not, Sarah. Unless you work with me, you won't be free to walk the streets until you're in your fifties or later. Trust me on that."

"Bullshit. How could you pull that off? You guys aren't Gods. You can't make people disappear."

"These," Rod said and shoved a manila folder across the table at her. He stepped away from the table and started pacing in front of the door.

She flipped the folder open. Inside sat a series of pictures. The first one was the image of a man who looked to be in his early twenties. He was clearly dead, his eyes wide open, slack jaw, body askew. She knew he wasn't sleeping. Too much blood. Someone had stabbed the guy in the stomach in a crude attempt to offer him a free vivisection.

The next picture was more of the same. Different angles exposed every gruesome detail of a life exterminated.

"What's this got to do with me?"

"That's Joseph Singer. He was murdered by his girlfriend, who has never been located. Until now."

Sarah looked up at him. Rod stopped pacing and knocked

on the two-way glass. A moment later, four men entered the room, two of them carrying machine guns strapped across their shoulders.

"What do you mean, until now?" Sarah asked, her mouth barely moving. She started to put it all together.

"I have multiple witnesses who will place you at the scene of the murder. Joseph's sister saw a picture of you and will testify in court that you were the Sarah that Joseph Singer was dating at the time of his murder. I have enough proof and numerous witnesses to bury you with this charge and get a first-degree murder conviction which will keep you behind bars for a very long time." He stopped and crossed his arms, staring down at her. "Think on these things, Sarah."

Real fear set in. She had killed before. Many times, but they were all in self-defense. She had never committed the act of murder for the sake of murder itself. Although she could make an exception with killing Rod. It would be a pleasure.

Her bladder tightened. She needed to pee. She needed to think. She couldn't show weakness. But who really cared now? Did Rod think he could toss this at her and nail her to his cross? She had to admit, his play was solid, but it wasn't checkmate yet.

"I've never heard of Joseph Singer. The charge is bullshit, and you know it. Others will, too. We both know I've killed before, but those people deserved to die. You have nothing on me."

"We're talking about a college kid here. A jury will eat this up. No amount of pleading will offer a reasonable doubt to them with the case I've got. But, Sarah, help me, work with me, and this Joseph Singer case goes away."

"You're delusional, you know that. You're fucking gone. Loco, crazy, whatever … you're just fucked. You can't ruin people's lives like this. It's unconscionable."

Rod stepped toward his men and the door behind them. "Sarah, you may be a hero to the public with your recent media exposure, but they don't know about Joseph. This case will bury you. Forever."

"I have no idea what you're talking about, riddle man. I didn't do this," she said, gesturing at the pictures.

Rod stopped at the door, his hand on the knob. "You haven't figured out who you're dealing with yet, have you? That's a mistake. Know your enemy, Sarah, know your enemy."

Sarah looked away, her headache all but forgotten as the Advil had done its job. She sat on the verge of tears.

A nightmare. That's what her life had become. The more she helped people, it seemed the worse things got. The stakes had risen, and she wasn't sure she could deal with it. What if Rod really did charge her with the murder of Joseph Singer and led her away to face a courtroom? It would take years to deal with something as serious as murder. Could she ever shake it? And what about Drake? He was to be shot later in the day, and there was nothing she could do about it because she was in Chicago, and he was in Toronto. Ultimately, Rod has killed Drake by bringing her here.

Who's the real murderer now, asshole?

Rod stood by the door, surrounded by his bodyguards. How many men made him feel secure around her?

"I know who I'm dealing with," she said. "An asshole."

"That's right, Sarah. Call me names. No problem, but remember this. You've seen what I can do with a commercial airliner in federal airspace. A simple murder cover-up is the next face on a milk carton, filed as a missing persons indefinitely. Refuse me, and I'll see you go down for first-degree murder. Work with me, and in a few years, you'll have more freedom to move about. Maybe one day you'll even get married." He stopped talking, covered his mouth as he chuckled, and opened the door. "Sorry about that. I wouldn't want to joke about something that'll never happen. Sarah Roberts, married … imagine that."

Then he stepped from the room, followed by his men, and slammed the door shut.

They left in time to miss her tears.

Chapter 4

DRAKE BELLAMY SLOWLY GOT out of Spencer's police-issued, unmarked car and stepped in line at the ticket office. A light breeze ruffled his hair. It proved to be a great day. Spencer Milton had called yesterday and offered to take him to the Blue Jay game at the Rogers Centre in downtown Toronto. Drake had accepted as only recently he had been out of the hospital and mobile again. After what Monika and her brothers had put him through, he was lucky to be alive. He had a broken wrist, a bullet wound in his left arm, and two minor wounds on his left leg that caused a slight limp. Other than the cast on his arm, which wouldn't come off for a few more weeks, and his limp, he was healing fast.

Spencer had spent a lot of time at the hospital with him, taking his statement and piecing everything together step by step. Eventually, they got closer, bonding over the ordeal. They had talked about sports. Drake wanted to golf again before the summer was out, and Spencer wanted to catch a few ball games.

When Spencer called him yesterday, he'd accepted and just now realized how lucky he was, standing in the warm Toronto sun, anticipating a cold beer and a hot dog, a good game and companionship with the lead cop on the case who saved his life a few weeks ago.

He took in a deep breath and thanked God he was still standing. Two weeks ago, he was shot and about to be kicked off the edge of a cliff, but Spencer had shown up in time. Drake had picked up a baseball bat and broke the shooter's head as bullets zinged by him.

He laughed. A baseball bat stopped the madness, and here he was, about to watch the game of baseball.

Weird how shit works out.

A hand slapped his shoulder, and he jumped.

"I found a great spot up close for the car," Spencer said as he joined him in line. "Wow, slow lineup." He looked at his watch. "We still have over an hour before the game starts."

"Spencer, I wanted to thank you for taking me out to the ball game today."

"Whoa, you gonna start singing?"

"No, no, just, it feels good to be out again."

Spencer stepped back a little and faced Drake. "You almost got killed. It's about time you started living."

"I know, I know, but it's over. What I have to live with now is the threat of Ferenci. He left me that note, and no one has been able to find him. He could be anywhere, lurking around with a gun, anxious to put a few holes in me."

"We have guys looking for him as we speak. I'm here with you, and I'm armed. You're safe. Everything will be okay."

"I'm excited about this … so why do I feel spooked?" Drake asked as the line moved forward. "I know this is my first time in public again, but it's over, right?"

Spencer tapped him on the shoulder. "I've got your back."

They made it to the ticket window, bought their tickets, and started for the doors.

"We got great seats," Spencer said. "We're about eight rows up from the third baseline. This'll be awesome."

They entered the stadium and walked through security, Spencer showing his detective ID. After collecting a couple of beers and hotdogs, they made their way toward the seats.

Drake's uneasy feeling increased. There were too many people. It felt like some of them were staring at him. He'd seen uniformed officers walking among the patrons, too.

"Spencer, why are there so many uniformed cops here?"

"That's normal at a major event like this. They hire them for security." He stopped talking to drink from his beer cup. "You'll see them out on the field, too. Quite common. Nothing to worry about. There's been no call for beefed-up security. This is completely normal."

Drake took a long swallow of his Canadian Ice beer and followed Spencer to their seats. They walked down the concrete steps until they reached their row, edged in, and sat down.

The field seemed massive, as was the roof, which sat open for the game. Drake was happy he'd brought his sunglasses. The sun beat down on them and would continue to for the next few hours.

Maybe I should've brought sunblock.

Spencer looked at his watch. "The game doesn't start for

another forty-five minutes yet. Once it does start, if those two seats four rows up aren't taken, we're moving closer to the action. Deal?"

"Deal."

He should be having a blast, but the ominous feeling wouldn't abate. Something bothered him deeper than his reluctance to come out in public after what had happened to him just weeks ago.

It was like someone was watching him. Would today be the day Ferenci tried to kill him as he had threatened two weeks ago? Would Spencer be able to stop it?

Drake took another long gulp of his beer and decided to let it go. He'd never be able to enjoy the game if he constantly thought about Ferenci. That part of his life was over. The cops would pick up Ferenci. Everything would work out.

Drake saw he had almost finished his beer.

"Spencer, I'm going to head back up and grab another one. It went down too quick."

"Get me one, too," Spencer said, handing Drake a twenty. "If I'm not here when you get back, I'll be in those two seats up ahead."

"Got it," Drake said and headed up the stairs.

His shoulders shuddered with the distinct feeling of being watched.

Chapter 5

ELMORE GOT TO THE bottom of the stairs and stopped. He admired what he'd created. Two cages, both with vertical bars for a door, the walls made of concrete blocks he'd piled to the roof. He couldn't believe he had done so well. Over two years of having multiple women and not a single problem. No police nosing around. Not a single escapee.

And there never will be. My house is a fortress.

Jackie lay on the cot, wrapped in the thin blanket he allowed her to have. He smiled at the thought of the fun they'd had, but it was time for her to go. She disgusted him now. She had brought this on. It was her fault. Having to deal with her caused him stress. If only she'd been better, nicer.

Why couldn't you have been stronger? Like a Sarah? I might have kept you longer.

He stepped closer to the bars and stared down at her. Under the thin sheet, she was dressed in panties. They were the only clothes any of his girls were allowed to wear. The panties were changed twice a day, then shipped out to men all over the globe who yearned for the smell of a woman. If Jackie only knew how much money she had made him, she would be surprised he had to dispose of her.

The table behind him had all the tools he'd need. Elmore stepped over to it, grabbed a book of matches and a nail clipper, and walked back to the cell door. He tore off one match, lit it, and then tossed it at Jackie. The lit match almost extinguished itself in flight but made it to her skin and flared out. Jackie moved a little in her sleep.

He tore off three matches, lit all of them together, and tossed the trio at her. This batch stayed aflame better and landed on her ankle. It burned bright for a moment—then Jackie jumped and screamed.

They never seem to get used to the burning.

Jackie got to her feet and stood in the middle of her cell, staring at him. She would be afraid as this wasn't a normal visit. The clock on the cell wall had a purpose. He came with breakfast, and he came with dinner. Then he came at nine in the evening, on the dot, every night, and they were to be ready for him. With dinner, Jackie received a wet cloth, enough water to bathe, and a new pair of panties. She would pay dearly for one odor, one speck of dirt on her person. She had learned early. Pain was a serious motivator.

Elmore held the nail clipper out until it reached between the bars. Jackie hesitated for only a moment, then stepped closer in her bare feet and took the clipper.

Without a word, she attended to her fingernails. He'd been letting her grow them lately as her time with him was coming to a close.

The thrill of a new girl always stirred things in him that a girl of six months could never do. He would grab one this week or next week from the studio. It would be easy. The stupid girls put themselves out there, naïve and vulnerable, almost announcing to the world that they want to be taken.

They show up at his studio to do a photo shoot in a pair of panties. During the shoot, they spill their life story. Mother doesn't love them, family disowned them, living on the streets or with friends. No one knows they're there, but they needed some quick cash. He butters them up and offers a premium contract for the studio north of Toronto. To consider the job, they could come and see the studio. After agreeing, they end up in his cage. The cameras at L'Amore Studio would show the photo shoot, how professional it was, and then the girl getting paid and leaving. What the camera doesn't show is the girl walking out to the alley and getting in his car. No camera, or no one, ever set eyes on them again.

Jackie had been so easy. A clean girl who had been kicked out of her boyfriend's house after a night of boozing. She'd explained to Elmore that her mother told her to not call begging for help if she ever shacked up with Mark. She'd had nowhere to turn. After three days in a shelter, Jackie had applied for the photo shoot, and within two hours, she had been locked in Elmore's cage.

The girl before Jackie got a fast execution. Elmore gave her a farewell hour of forced sex while Jackie was made to watch from her cage, and then he slit her throat. He remembered it distinctly because of how much blood there had been. It made him angry to no end that she could bleed that much all over his clean floor. It took him two days to get the cell clean to the exact standard he expected from his hostages.

During those two days, he'd forgotten all about feeding

Jackie. He had heard her cries and her pleas but ignored them as his anger overrode any sense of humanity.

And now it was Jackie's turn. At least the next girl would be spared Jackie's final moments.

She finished with her fingernails and collected them all without dropping a single one as previously instructed. Jackie stepped closer to the bars and reached out to Elmore. He took the nails and examined them.

Good. A great batch that'll immortalize Jackie, at least for the next month or so.

He looked back at her near-naked form and nodded toward her feet. Jackie looked down and understood. She bent to her knee and started in on her toenails. Once each foot was clipped, she handed all those nails to Elmore, who took his loot and stepped to the table to place them in a small bowl where they'd be washed and ready for his teeth at a later date.

He stood back in front of her cell and pointed at the only piece of clothing she wore.

The panties.

Again, without pause, she understood and slowly slipped them off, not allowing them to touch the floor.

Elmore could see the worried look on her face, and he knew why. Since this wasn't his regular visit and he hadn't supplied her with the requisite cloth to bathe with, would he use her body as he always did? She wouldn't be as clean if he did, which was never good for Elmore.

He understood. But that was the only way to deal with filth. He had to get down and dirty to root filth out. He needed to lay with her as the unclean thing she was, and then he could be angry enough to remove the stain that she was from his world.

Jackie handed him her last pair of panties. He laid them down in the box that would be shipped out in the morning with the pictures he'd taken of her earlier that authenticated the use of the panties.

If the customers who bought the underwear ever knew how authentication was attained, he wondered how many would continue to purchase them.

Jackie stood in the center of her little prison, naked, shivering with fear, not cold, looking pathetic.

How dare you? Come here and act like you're someone special. I will teach you what's special.

Other than the little mattress he allowed them as a cot and the small thin sheet for a blanket, there was a waterless toilet and nothing else in the cell. He couldn't allow them any way to off themselves. He also had to be careful that they wouldn't discover a weapon to attack him with when he entered their cells for his evening pleasure.

Elmore pulled the cell keys from his pocket and found the one for Jackie's door. For a moment, the room blurred in his vision. It was always this way. His anger would rise and become a fury. In that final moment, all that mattered was the girl and removing the stain that she had become.

"No, no …" Jackie whimpered and stepped away from the door.

"Why no, Jackie? After six months, you're used to me by now."

"Not at this hour. You never come in the afternoon."

"Am I required to check with you when I want to alter the schedule?"

The lock clicked, and the cell door opened. He eased it

open all the way. At any other moment, she would be pretty —gorgeous. One hundred and thirty pounds, tanned skin, nice cup size, and long, pretty hair. Two, three months ago, she was. He had enjoyed her labors. But now she was dirty, unclean. What Elmore did with grime was wipe it out.

"No. I just … what I mean is, I'm scared."

"It'll be okay, Jackie. After today, we are done here."

It must be akin to how cows feel when being led to the slaughterhouse. An innate sense of impending doom. They know their fate and are powerless to stop it. In Jackie's eyes, the acceptance that her time had come clouded them. But Jackie wasn't a cow. She acted more like a squirrel stuck in a corner as a large attacker advanced. The violence he detected coming off her in waves surprised him.

He stood three feet from her when she raised her hands to ward him off.

"No, please, I'll do whatever you ask."

Nothing in Elmore that would be considered rational heard a word she had said. All he felt, all he saw, and all he desired was an end to her. An end to the fake relationship she had made him conduct with her. An end to the wondering if someone would knock on his front door looking for her. An end. That's what Elmore needed now.

Jackie moved to the back wall as Elmore edged closer. He brought his hands to the lip of his underwear and slowly lowered the pair to his ankles. Now with his member exposed, it hardened further with anticipation.

Then Jackie sprung. Off the wall, she flew at him with the violence of Tie Domi in his prime.

Elmore hadn't expected it. She caught him off balance. He faltered and stepped backward until he hit the bars.

Jackie's small fist smacked him in the face, then the mouth. His response delayed, she ran past him and headed for the stairs, her flesh barely bouncing as she'd lost weight in the time she'd spent with Elmore.

He let her go, wiping at the blood that had started to seep from his split lip.

"This is going to cost you," Elmore shouted.

Jackie made it to the top of the stairs. What she didn't know was that Elmore had locked the metal door behind him, and the only way out was with the key he held in his pocket.

He picked up his underwear, slid them back on, and stepped from the cell. The pain made him angry, not horny. Jackie still had to be removed, but now it wouldn't be because she had made him filthy with her feminine touch but because she had hurt him.

"It's time to pay for your misdeeds."

"Noooo," Jackie screamed from the top of the stairs.

"Stupid bitch," he said as he looked at his table of tools. A handsaw, a screwdriver, and many other devices she could've used as a weapon sat out in the open. Instead, she had run for the stairs. That was the female condition. Just being born was enough to fuck them up.

He chose the Craftsman screwdriver. If he weren't going to screw her, he'd let his tool do it for him.

Jackie remained at the top of the stairs, shivering, crying, her arms wrapped around her nakedness.

It was a sight he would remember. Jackie had served him well.

"Goodbye, Jackie."

Elmore started up the stairs, one slow step at a time. His tongue came out and tasted the blood on his lip as it clotted, the slight sting of the punch lingering.

On the fourth step, Jackie sprang into action. He'd advanced slowly. Based on her performance in the cage, he had expected it.

Jackie screamed like a feline in a full fight with another as she jumped two stairs and dove at Elmore. He braced himself and lifted the long screwdriver, aiming for the center of her chest.

It connected cleanly and entered her ribs between her breasts. Her weight drove Elmore back until they both fell. The hard basement floor proved unforgiving. He hit his elbow hard enough to cause pins and needles to course through his left hand.

But Jackie hit harder. She smacked down and rolled onto her back, her mouth bleeding after making contact with the floor directly. A couple of teeth had cut through her lip. She rolled her head back and forth, moaning, crying, and trying to figure out what had happened to her chest.

He watched as she lifted her head and realized the screwdriver's handle stuck out of her skin. Her breathing became more and more labored.

Elmore got up slowly and moved closer. Her eyes were wide, her nostrils flaring in their feeble attempt to claim as much air as they could catch. But it was no use. Blood began to slip past her lips. She was dying, and there was nothing she could do about it.

Elmore looked up and down her body, once pretty, now broken and dirty. He wadded up a gob of saliva and spit on her stomach.

"That's what I think of vermin, you fucking whore."

He reached over and laid his palm around the

screwdriver's handle. Both her hands came up to his wrist, and her head shook back and forth fast, her eyes wide. She tried to say something but only screamed as Elmore twisted the tool in and out.

Jackie's body convulsed, her hands fell away, and her eyes rolled back in her head.

In her last moment, her bowels evacuated.

"Oh, man, you are going to pay for that. I cannot believe you soiled my floor."

Elmore got up, fished for the keys in his shirt pocket, and headed for the stairs. He would clean up in his bathroom, get dressed in his plastic coveralls and grab a bag of lime from the garage.

Then he'd return, take Jackie apart with his handsaw and start planting her in the field behind his house, lime coating every piece.

No trace of Jackie would ever be found. The basement would take some cleaning, but he'd get on it and then start searching for Sarah Roberts again.

One day he'd find her. When that day came, he'd be ready.

If he couldn't find her soon, he'd answer the resumes he had received for photo shoots and find another young girl to keep as a toy until he found Sarah.

Whatever happened, his needs came first, and nothing or no one would stop him.

Not even someone as courageous and heroic as Sarah Roberts.

On the stairs, he stopped and said to himself, "Sarah, I'm coming for you."

Chapter 6

SSARAH'S HEADACHE HAD COMPLETELY dissipated, but the back of her neck still hurt where the stitches were. While waiting for Rod to return, she had paced the room, tried to see through the two-way glass, and knocked on the door enough times to make her knuckles red. Normally she would take the time they wanted to sweat her with ease, but Drake's life hung in the balance. It was decision time. She had to do something. She couldn't let Rod murder Drake simply because he had an agenda.

She knocked on the glass. "Deal time. Get Rod in here. He's got one minute, or the deal is off the table. And when I say off the table, I mean for good."

Sarah sat back in the chair and placed both hands in front of her. She felt anger that Drake could be killed so easily— just because she was stuck in Chicago. Why was she the only one who really cared?

After what felt like a minute had passed, she looked back at the glass. She couldn't believe it. The door hadn't opened.

Now she felt her anger rising to dangerous levels.

"What are you doing here?" she asked, slamming her hands down on the top of the table where she sat. "If you want to see what I can do, get Rod in here. Now!"

She never bluffed. This had to be it. No deal. She couldn't be certain without a clock, but it sure felt like a minute had gone by.

The door opened. Rod stood there.

"They said you wanted to talk."

"We're running out of time. Sit. Listen to what I have to say."

Rod stepped in and shut the door. He checked the knob to ensure it held the door tight and walked over to the table. After crossing his arms, he stared down at her and waited.

"I'm going to tell you some shit, but not because I want to and not because you made me. Because it's the right thing to do." She paused and waited for a reaction. Rod stood like a stone statue. "I received a message in Hungary from my dead sister. That's why I came to Toronto. There's someone I have to save. I'm prepared to make a deal, but it has to be on my terms. It won't work unless I run the show."

Rod shook his head. "No way. Talk first. Then I'll decide what'll be done."

She was clean out of options. He held the control, and they both knew it. She had to go forward with this and deal with the consequences later. Another man's life was at stake.

"His name is Drake Bellamy. He knows too much about the immigration fraud group that is being dismantled in Europe and around the world as we speak. He has been ordered killed. My sister told me where and when. I'm sure she'll give me more details as the time gets closer."

"Forget it," Rod said and turned back to the door.

"Wait. You can't just walk away. If you do, you're no better than the shooter."

"I may not be, but I'll be smarter."

"How do you figure?"

"Letting you out of this facility means you'll escape. I can't keep trying to lock you down. Believe it or not, that takes a lot of effort."

Sarah stood too fast, the back of her knees knocking the chair over. "Rod, an innocent man will die this afternoon if you don't act. I will show you how my gift works. Isn't that what you want? Isn't that why you brought me here and expended all that effort? Come on, work with me."

He turned around to fully face her, crossing his arms again. "Then keep talking. Sell me on this idea of yours."

"There will be questions you'll have to answer, Rod."

"Like what?"

"There were people who were supposed to meet me at the airport in Toronto. After two days, they'll be going ballistic, trying to figure out where I am. It won't take them long to come snooping for you."

"By people, you mean Parkman. And that doesn't matter because, officially, I don't exist. There's nothing that a cop like Parkman could ever do that'll get through the layers of bullshit my organization remains protected under."

"Then what is the purpose? You tell me. If you brought me here to examine my talents, why aren't we doing just that? Otherwise, this is nothing better than glorified kidnapping."

Neither spoke. They stared at each other. Sarah waited. She wasn't going to break the silence first.

Rod uncrossed his arms and walked back to the table. "I'm listening."

"Drake is supposed to be at a baseball game this afternoon. The hit should happen near the end of the game. He will be shot in the face for exposing people in the immigration ring. Some of those people, along with a few innocents, were killed in Toronto recently. I got this from Vivian. I always try to do what Vivian tells me to do. That's why I'm still alive."

Rod placed his hands on the wooden table. "Okay, thank you. Now we can see if your prophecy comes true, and we don't have to go anywhere. Thanks, Sarah." He stepped away and opened the door to leave.

"Wait!" Sarah shouted. "Fuck, are you ever a hard man to deal with. Are you saying you'll let the shooting happen just to prove I knew about it?"

Rod faced her. Two men stood in the hallway behind him. From where she sat, she could see they were heavily armed.

"No, I'm going to alert the Canadian authorities and tell them everything you just said. That'll give them," he paused and looked at his watch. "About three hours to locate Drake in the ballpark and remove him. That will save his life. I'll have them look for a shooter. In the meantime, start giving me more prophecies to work with."

"What if they don't find the shooter?" Sarah asked. "They'll detain Drake, and nothing will happen. Then, two days later, the shooter catches Drake at a delicatessen buying a fucking sandwich and shoots him in the face spilling lettuce and ham all over the fucking place. You're still the murderer in that case because you had a chance to stop it yourself by finding Drake and staying close to him, and having me there. If you don't catch the shooter today, he'll try again tomorrow. You know that, and I know that."

Rod looked at each man flanking him and then turned back to Sarah. She tapped her hand on the table, frustrated by his inability to see it her way.

"Look," Sarah continued for her last try. "The information I receive is quite accurate. You know where the shooter will be. The chances of nailing him today are much greater than on any other day. If we do exactly as Vivian says, everything will work out."

Rod shook his head again in that irritating way; his forehead lowered, his eyes looking up at her.

"Everything will work out? Like how it all worked out with Gert four years ago. You almost got yourself killed, like how it worked out with those guys who kept you prisoner in a small shed. You were shot a couple of times. In the temple at the compound, you were about to be raped and murdered, but Parkman had trailed you and walked in just at the right time. But everything will work out, right Sarah? And I work for NASA and take routine flights to Mars to negotiate territorial rights for oil in their tar pits." He stepped into the corridor. "No go. No lies. No deceptions. No more bullshit. Just prophecies. Do that, and maybe we'll feed you today."

"Rod, wait," Sarah said, her arm extended. "You can't seriously do this."

"Just did."

He pulled the door shut. The lock clicked.

She righted the chair, sat on it, and lowered her head to the table. "I'm sorry, Drake. I tried. I fucking tried."

***

The door burst open, and Sarah jumped in her seat. She'd almost nodded off.

"What's going on?" she asked.

Rod stood there with at least six men behind him.

"We're going," he said. "I've changed my mind. Get up."

"Going where?" she asked.

"The stadium in Toronto. A plane is ready to take us."

Her head spun in circles as she loosened her neck. "What are you saying? We may be too late already."

"We will be if you keep hesitating."

She didn't need any more prompting. Sarah got up and ran to them.

Rod held something out. "Here, put this on first."

"What's that?"

"A GPS tracking bracelet. Whenever you leave this facility, you will wear one of these the whole time. I will never have you out of my sight again."

"Okay, fair enough," Sarah nodded. "But you stay out of my way at the stadium. I do it on my terms."

"Agreed."

Sarah extended her hand, and Rod secured the bracelet on her wrist. She wondered why he had a change of heart.

"The tracking bracelet beams a signal to a van that I'll have parked outside the stadium. Even if you manage to escape our clutches, we'll always know where you are. Are we clear?"

Sarah nodded.

"You're not giving me much time to organize this. There's paperwork whenever you enter another country.

While I made you wait, I got the plane ready and organized everything as much as possible."

With Sarah running in the midst of the group, all seven men headed down the corridor and up two flights of concrete stairs. A door led them outside, where Sarah had to close her eyes at the bright sun and blink rapidly to see where to go. A waiting Lear jet sat, its engines already running.

"We're landing at the Toronto Island Airport," Rod shouted to be heard over the noise of the jets. "Do you realize how hard this was on such short notice?"

"You managed to rearrange the flight plan of a major airliner and have it land in Chicago. I'm sure a little ball game in Toronto isn't too hard for a man of your talents. Come on, it couldn't be that hard. They're Canadians."

"What does that mean?"

"They're nice people up there. They're pushovers."

They got to the plane's door. Two men jumped in and waited for Sarah. She looked at Rod. "Just remember. Stay out of my way. This is my gig. Get me to the stadium. I'll handle the rest."

"That's what I'm worried about."

Chapter 7

THE BALL GAME WAS in full swing as the black SUV pulled up to the Rogers Centre. On the quick drive to the Rogers Centre from the Island Airport, Rod explained that the Toronto Police already had a group of uniformed officers posted throughout the complex. Along with that, they sent over five plainclothes officers to help in the event a shooting occurred. All Toronto officers had been given a picture of Sarah. They all knew to allow her full access to all areas of the building and help if she needed anything.

"Okay, Sarah, here's a couple of pieces of paper and a pen in case Vivian gets in contact. Listen, I'll be out of sight but watching you the whole time. That bracelet will tell us where you are. Remove it, and the consequences will be severe. Got it."

Sarah grabbed the paper and pen. "We're running out of time," she said, holding the door handle with her other hand. Ever since they'd landed at the Island Airport, she'd watched for Parkman to show up. She was sure she'd see him soon as he was probably still in Toronto, looking for her. The Lear jet had made the flight in just over an hour. The ball game was in the seventh inning, and according to the radio, the Jays were behind four runs. None of that mattered. All that mattered to Sarah was getting into the stadium and locating Drake as soon as possible.

"I need to hear it," Rod said. "All bets are off if you remove that bracelet. I will take you back to the States and have you charged with the murder of Joseph Singer. A radio transmitter embedded in the bracelet is programmed to send a distress signal as soon as it's tampered with. A simple pair of scissors can cut this one with the proper amount of strength, which is difficult with one hand. But—be warned … don't. Deal?"

Sarah glared at him. "Deal. Now, let me go, or Drake will be shot, and that'll void any deals we're sitting around here making. We didn't come all this way to chat."

Rod looked past her and nodded. The door clicked to unlock. She opened it and ran for the gate, her ALL ACCESS pass dangling around her neck. Just before she reached the door, she turned and looked up at the massive structure of the CN Tower and marveled at its height and how thin it looked. Then she entered the stadium through gate seven.

Rod had asked how she'd know Drake. Tickets for the ball game were purchased, and seat numbers were allotted, but not by the person's name, like a plane seat. If Drake used a credit card, maybe they could find the purchase and trace it back to a seat number, but that sort of thing took time, and so far, Rod's people were coming up empty. Sarah had explained that all she was supposed to do was show up. Vivian would handle the rest. There was a process, and she trusted in that.

She stepped past a group of slow-moving people and hustled into the circular hallway, beyond which she saw a gigantic stadium filled with seats and thousands of baseball fans.

"How am I expected to locate one man in all that?"

The Toronto Police were supposed to step in once she found Drake. They had been informed that Drake was a suspect in a high-level criminal investigation in the States, and Sarah was helping them locate him through a positive ID. All the extra noise Rod had created around Drake had made her mad. The cops might be watching her too closely. The shooter could see the extra police presence. Anything could happen to screw this up, and it would all fall on her head.

She had to do something about it, and she had to do it fast.

Sarah looked both ways until she saw the ladies' bathroom sign. She ran toward it, hoping Vivian was close. In the bathroom, she picked a stall at the back, closed the door, and latched it.

With the paper and pen in her hand, she sat on the closed toilet and leaned into the side wall so that if she passed out, she wouldn't hit the floor.

"Come on, Vivian," she whispered. "Give me something."

Sarah felt the familiar stirrings in her writing hand as if on cue. She laid her head back and closed her eyes. A moment later, she opened them and saw a note in her own handwriting.

Drake's in blue seat 126. The third baseline. The bullet

will be shot in fifteen minutes. The shooter is a man named Ferenci. He has help.

At the bottom was an afterword. Like Vivian had remembered something.

Beware the cop. He's fake. He wants to kill you.

Sarah reread the note at least three times. All she had to do was find Drake's seat, and she still had over ten minutes. She recalled something Rosalie had said to her in Montone, Italy after the head of the immigration consortium had been killed just a few weeks ago. It would take over six months for the investigators to go through everything before they could possibly start arresting anyone. That meant people all over the world hadn't been exposed yet—they were still in business … doing business.

Then who is the cop that wants to kill me?

How many men could Ferenci have? Two, three, or more? Rod had four with him and five plainclothes cops, plus a stadium filled with uniforms. Which one was the cop she was supposed to watch out for? How would she know?

Too many questions that had to be answered at another time. Save Drake first, and then figure everything else out.

She opened the stall and walked out of the bathroom. As soon as she stepped into the wide corridor again, she realized that her escape plan was right in front of her.

Rod won't even know what hit him.

She couldn't believe it hadn't hit her earlier.

First, she had to get rid of the tracking bracelet.

She jogged along the corridor until she found a hotdog stand with a small line. On the side, down behind the booth, she saw an employee breaking down boxes from a shipment.

He held a pair of scissors.

Perfect.

The clock continued unabated. Time was short, but she had to remove the bracelet first for everything to work right.

She stepped up to the young guy who didn't look older than twenty.

"Excuse me, can I borrow those scissors?" she asked.

He stopped what he was doing, looked at the scissors, and then back at Sarah. She smiled and rolled a finger seductively down the length of her hair. "I just need them for a second."

The employee shrugged and handed the scissors over. Sarah took them, lifted her sleeve, and applied them to the bracelet.

"Hey, what's that? Is it one of those things you have to wear when you've broken the law?"

Sarah nodded. "Something like that."

After two tries, she still couldn't budge it. "Damn the fucking clock. I'm almost out of time."

The clerk had stepped back a few feet.

"Here," she gestured with the scissors. "Help me with this."

No one had noticed them yet. Since the baseball game was almost over, the hotdog stand wasn't as busy. People still walked by in the wide hallway, but no one looked at them.

"I can't help. That's illegal."

As fast as she could, Sarah stepped up, slipped her foot behind the guy's ankle, and pushed his shoulders back. He lost his balance and fell to the floor backward. She pounced down and landed beside him, the scissors at the base of his throat just above the collarbone.

"Don't scream. Don't do anything crazy, or these scissors

will enter your neck. Do you want to bleed out and die?"

She wondered what crime he was conjuring up that she would've committed by wearing the bracelet. This act of violence would fill his mind with many scenarios.

He shook his head in response to her question.

"Good, because I'm sick and tired of having to kill people."

His eyes widened as far as they could.

"After I kill you," Sarah continued, "they'll probably give me two of these fucking things. So, I'll make you a deal, cut this thing off, and you'll never see me again. Tell me you won't help, and I'll jam these scissors as far into your throat as I can. Cool?"

He nodded like an insane bobblehead figure. Sarah brought her wrist up and applied the scissors to the weakest part of the bracelet. She held one side of the scissor's grip so the hotdog stand employee couldn't turn them on her and waited. He inserted his fingers inside the grip and pushed. It took two strong attempts before the bracelet snapped in half.

Sarah got up and stepped back from him. She tossed the bracelet in a corner and then threw the scissors after them.

"Thanks. Oh, and I was kidding about hurting you. I never would do that sort of thing." She smiled. "Have a good one."

She had to try to make him feel better. He looked like he had just shat his pants.

Sarah turned away and ran, looking for a clock. She still had to get to Drake's seat, which, based on how the colors worked, was coming up a hundred meters ahead.

The whole time she watched her back. Somewhere a cop wasn't to be trusted. She would hate to be gunned down because some asshole wanted her dead. Too bad her sister couldn't have been more specific about which cop she was supposed to be cautious of.

She reached the blues with less than five minutes left. She stopped at the top of the stairs that led down to Drake's seat and looked for any cops. Even though she hated them, and one was hunting her, she needed their help with Rod.

Two uniformed officers were walking her way, talking animatedly about something.

She ran over and stopped in front of them, making the two cops cease talking. They both took her face in and looked at each other.

"You recognize me? I was told all the cops here got my picture."

They nodded in unison. "How can we help?"

"You've all been had. The American, Rod Howley, is lying. He's the one behind everything. He's not the shooter, but I suspect he has ties to the shooter."

"The shooter? What are you talking about? We were told they were here to apprehend a suspect or a witness. That was it."

Sarah shook her head. "No, listen. A man is here to shoot someone named Drake. Because Howley is behind it, he used his influence to deflect the Toronto Police force. I don't want to be killed, but he has a gun, and someone will be shot within five minutes. Tell the rest of your men."

"Are you absolutely certain? I'm going to have to verify this story."

"Go ahead."

The older cop of the two stepped a few feet away and repeated on his radio what Sarah had said about a shooter and that a man was supposed to be shot.

At the right moment, with only minutes to spare, Sarah waited until a trio of baseball fans walked past them. She turned toward Drake's aisle and hit the stairs running as fast as she could, using the fans as cover.

The crowd roared as someone at bat hit the ball. She couldn't look up, or she'd fall down the wide stairs. A quick glance at the seats told her she had about ten rows left.

Down to a minute, she slowed her pace and started looking ahead at all the people watching the game in their seats. Two uniformed officers were running along the front rows, heading toward the bottom of the stairs she was on. It relieved her to see that she'd make Drake's seat before they even started up.

Three rows away now. She slowed and looked behind her. The two cops she'd stopped were coming down the stairs after her.

Shit. This is unwinding too fast.

With cops running at her from both directions and time running out, Sarah stepped up to Drake's row and scanned the seat numbers until she saw seat number 126.

It was empty.

Chapter 8

DRAKE WATCHED THE ACTION on the field with a lack of interest. This was his first time back in public since his life had been turned upside down. He thought he'd be dead or spending the rest of his life in prison for what happened two weeks ago. But now a lot of other people were dead, and he was watching a baseball game with a police officer.

Even though that made him shake his head at how strange the world could be, he still couldn't shake the feeling of being watched.

The bat cracked out a ball that looked like it might be a home run. The crowd went wild, with people all over the stadium jumping to their feet. Drake stayed seated beside Spencer.

"Things are really getting heated up, eh?" Drake said.

Spencer nodded. "You enjoying the game?"

"Sure."

"It doesn't look like it."

"I'm just feeling a little off."

"I hope you're still not worried about Ferenci. You can't put your life on hold because maybe this guy is after you."

Drake looked down at his hands as he fiddled with the white cast that covered his knuckles. "You're right. It's just, those Hungarians are non-stop. I don't think it'll end until they're all dead."

Spencer slapped Drake's leg. "Don't worry a second more. We're on it."

The fans settled down as the ball went foul. Drake scanned the crowd. Two police officers ran along the front row. He watched as they hit the stairs that led toward them and started up.

"I wonder what that's all about," Drake said, pointing at the cops.

"Who knows?" Spencer said.

Drake could hear the inquisitive cop voice in Spencer. He wanted to know what was going on as much as Drake did.

The announcer came over the loudspeaker and announced they were looking for an escaped prisoner.

The Sony JumboTron lit up with a picture of a gorgeous blonde girl. Drake stared at it and frowned. He'd seen her before somewhere.

Then he remembered: The newspaper on the train two weeks ago when he headed to his grandparents' house in Oshawa. The front cover featured a girl who had exposed some kind of kidnapping ring at a Mormon Temple somewhere in the States.

The girl, he remembered from the *Toronto Sun* newspaper, was considered a hero. Her name eluded him at the moment.

The cops down below were coming up the stairs fast.

Drake turned in his seat and saw two cops running down the stairs heading his way, too.

Without turning back around, he said, "Hey, Spencer, something's definitely going on."

Then he looked at a girl standing two seats over and four rows up. She stared at the seats they had vacated.

As the announcer repeated the message about an escaped prisoner, the girl turned, and Drake remembered her name.

Sarah Roberts.

He saw her face. She looked up at the JumboTron, an expression of shock mixed with anger crossed her lovely features.

"Be right back," Drake said and jumped from his seat.

Sarah had turned away and stared up the steps at the approaching officers.

Drake stepped in behind her and tapped her shoulder.

Chapter 9

SARAH TURNED AT THE sound of "escaped prisoner" as it was shouted from the stadium's speakers. Her live image was plastered on the huge screen. She couldn't believe it. Rod must've got the call that she had removed her bracelet, and when the Toronto Police radioed in that there would be a shooting, he had ordered her taken back into custody.

He was attempting to stop her while she was still in sight. Having the JumboTron track her movements and plaster her image for everyone in the stadium to see was something she hadn't expected.

Rod, you are so full of tricks.

She turned to look at the cops approaching from above. They were only three rows away now and slowing down.

A hand touched her shoulder.

She jumped, spun around, and pulled the guy's wrist down, twisting it on the way around.

"Sarah, wait!"

She stopped. The man in front of her wasn't a cop, and it

wasn't Rod. He had a cast on the wrist she didn't grab.

Lucky for him.

"Why did you sneak up behind me, use my name, and touch me?" she asked. "Who are you?"

The guy stood at his full height. "Hello, Sarah Roberts. I'm Drake Bellamy. Pleased to meet you." He said all this with a huge smile, his eyes lit up, and his teeth perfect. She hadn't seen a man so gorgeous in all her life.

What horrible timing.

"Get down!" she shouted and grabbed his shoulders, shoving him to the stairs, mindful of his cast.

A crack like the sound of a whip and a snapping of broken wood resounded close to her head. Then another. She chanced a peek. The officers who had come down the stairs were lying down, flat out. Blood seeped from a leg wound on the cop closest to her.

"I told you Rod was part of the shooting," she shouted at the cop.

Even though the cop was wounded, he lifted his lapel radio and began speaking into it.

"Constable Jerkins here. I've been hit. Officer down. Sarah Roberts is not the problem. I repeat, Sarah Roberts is not the problem. We have a shooter aiming at us. We're under fire. Backup needed."

Great. Eat shit, Rod. I got you this time.

Another crack snapped a piece off the plastic chair beside Drake's head.

"What the hell is going on?" Drake shouted over the noise.

"Someone's trying to kill you. We have to get you out of here now."

"I'll help," someone said. "Come on."

Sarah looked up at the man who was offering a hand.

"That's Spencer," Drake said. "He's a cop. He's safe."

Sarah nodded and got to her feet. Spencer stood in front of Drake and guided them down the stairs.

The patrons close to Drake and Sarah were coming to their senses in the few seconds that the shooter got off two shots. The Sony JumboTron had been aimed at Sarah, so it caught her pulling Drake to the ground and the cop getting shot in the leg. Almost everyone in the building had watched, riveted by what they were seeing. Even the baseball players had stopped the game to watch.

Like the flip of a switch, the fans panicked. Almost like the wave conducted during a baseball game, people got up and ran for the stairs and the exits beyond. By the time Spencer, Drake, and Sarah had gone five rows down, a flow of people entered the stairs in mass hysteria, similar to a dam bursting.

Spencer pushed past as many as he could, yanking Drake through with him. The cops who had been coming up the stairs moved aside to allow Spencer room to pass.

In a pile of bodies, arms, and groping hands, Sarah stayed close to Drake. At the bottom of the stairs, Spencer jumped the small retainer wall and helped Drake over. Sarah cleared it with one jump off the last stair.

With all three of them on the turf, they were in the direct sun. Others had seen what they had done and followed them onto the turf. In seconds, running and screaming baseball fans rushed the field, running for the dugouts and exits with the wanton abandon that only having a gunman in their midst could cause.

Sarah stayed close to Drake as they all ran across the field. She couldn't let him out of her sight. He was her witness that he'd been shot at. If Rod somehow got his way, she would at least like to prove what she does works.

Beware the cop.

Sarah remembered the message from her sister. Could Spencer be the cop that wanted to kill her? That would make sense because Drake was at the ball game with Spencer. Maybe he brought Drake to the game to hand him over to the shooter.

Without any way to be sure, she had to play it safe. She followed close and waited for her opportunity.

They neared a large door that sat open, people exiting through it to the outside. It felt like they were running with half the people of Toronto on their tail.

At the last second, before they exited the stadium, Sarah grabbed Drake's right arm and leaned in close. "Come this way. Trust me, or you'll die."

She yanked him to the side and lost Spencer in the crowd within seconds. More than twenty heads separated Drake and Sarah from Spencer when he turned around and tried to locate them. She ducked her head and got Drake to bow at the waist.

Twenty feet into the new corridor, she spotted another exit sign.

"This way."

Sarah cautiously opened the door, which was unobstructed, and led to the outside. They stepped into the summer sun and walked away from the stadium with no one on their tail and no one knowing where they were.

Chapter 10

ELMORE DIPPED THE MOP in the bucket and continued scrubbing the basement floor. With each swing of the mop, he collected more blood, slowly removing proof that Jackie had ever been in his home. Later he'd wear protective clothing and use various bleaches and ammonia to finish cleaning her cell. The mattress would be burned, and every piece of clothing he wore. Not a single CSI unit would ever be able to prove Elmore used the cages for anything other than role-play with his panty photos that he shipped out weekly, which was a licensed, legitimate business.

He wondered how Sarah would hold up being locked away from the world. Maybe she would tell him things. Prophecies like she did for other people.

Jackie had been the longest girl he'd kept prisoner, coming in at six months. Maybe he'd keep Sarah longer. He could make an exception if she proved to be a good girl.

He had read a biography on the serial rapist and killer Ted Bundy and remembered Ann Rule's quote. Something about Ted being a sadistic sociopath who took pleasure in another human's pain and the control he had over his victims to the point of death and beyond. Elmore couldn't believe that. Of all the brilliant people he had read about, Ted was once married and functioned well. Sure he did mean things, but who didn't nowadays?

Elmore wasn't beyond caring. Some of the things he did were wrong, but he wasn't sadistic. He cared about his girls. They enjoyed their stay with him if they did what they were told. It proved to Elmore that he had the ability to care. He derived pleasure from their pain because they deserved it. Like disciplining a child—if necessary, so be it—he would enjoy teaching them.

He offered his girls the ability to control their future. If they did what was required of them, things got easier.

It was time to change the water in the bucket. Elmore lifted it and walked to the basement sink in the far corner.

What about Dali? What if he hadn't painted a single canvas? It would be interesting to see what a novel would have been like had Dali written instead. On the contrary, what if Edgar Allen Poe had only painted and never written a single word? How mad and dark would his paintings have been?

This, Elmore understood, described him. He was an artist of sorts. One that dealt with flesh and the human condition. Yet, he was brilliant because everyone had needs and yearned to fulfill them. For Elmore, it was easy because he simply took the needs that required fulfillment. That alone placed him above the rest.

With the bucket filled with fresh water, he returned to the area where Jackie had bled out.

He recalled the day when he was twelve, and his mother stopped him from painting images of women with injuries. He had explained that it showed fragility and beauty in one image. She had projected that he wanted to hurt women.

"Well, you were wrong, Mother dear," he said to the empty basement. "I didn't want to hurt women and never have. They do it to themselves. I'm only the messenger. The female condition has nothing to do with me."

He continued mopping and scrubbing for the next hour until it was time to take a break.

After cleaning his hands aggressively, he headed to his office and fired up his Mac, where he began his routine browsing. First, the financials of his vending machines in Japan. Then to Twitter to browse the newspapers that had defined his life.

Newspapers, the broadcasters of everyone's dirty laundry. Death and mayhem. When he was twelve, he read the local newspaper after he wasn't allowed to paint anymore, which completely redefined him. It soon became an obsession. Across Toronto, rape after rape took place and got front lines in the Toronto Sun Daily. It aroused him to read all the details of how a man had gone after what he had wanted and taken it. The truth, Elmore felt, was that it belonged to him. That was why women were created, and, at that early age, Elmore realized that he would one day be the same way. But he'd be smarter about it and ensure he never got arrested because it was socially unacceptable to have sex with a woman against her will. They enacted laws against it to protect women, yet it still happens daily. Politicians did it and got away with it. You could buy anything you wanted at the right price in large cities like Toronto. But Elmore would never pay. Paying for something you could take belittles the spender.

While waiting for the Toronto papers to load on his screen, he examined the last nails he'd ever get from Jackie. He placed them in the black container and closed it for later use.

With his right hand on the mouse, he used his left to pick at the scab on the side of his head and wondered what the next girl would look like. The excitement leading up to the caging of his next subject caused him to be permanently aroused.

"Days, it'll only be days, and then I'll have a plaything again," he whispered out loud.

Across the room, Sarah Roberts's face stared back from all the pictures he had plastered on the walls. He smiled at her and blew her a kiss.

"One day …"

The computer screen filled with the latest news.

The image of Sarah Roberts stared back at him from his monitor.

His eyes widened. The nail on his scab stopped scratching and pushed down on the piece he'd been working on.

The caption said there had been a stampede at the Rogers Centre, and the root of the problem had been American authorities' failed apprehension of one Sarah Roberts.

He couldn't believe it. The scab fell away in his fingers, and blood trickled down the side of his head.

This was his chance. Sarah Roberts had surfaced in Toronto. She was downtown. It couldn't have been set up better. If things went well, he could have her locked up before the end of the day.

He looked again at her face on the Sony JumboTron at the Rogers Centre.

"Yes. Sarah Roberts. That's you. How pretty."

American authorities. What do they want with her? Why are they up here in Canada hunting her?

He'd have to play that angle if he needed it.

He turned off his computer and headed upstairs to get dressed. He would finish cleaning the basement after he had Sarah. She took priority now.

He reveled in the odds. How was it possible that Sarah could be in Toronto?

He changed into his authentic Toronto Police uniform and donned a suit over that. He grabbed his police scanner off the bureau and got behind the wheel of his four-door sedan that resembled an unmarked cruiser with its Plexiglas shield between the front and back seats. He drove off his property with thoughts of Sarah.

"Sarah, it's only a matter of time now."

Chapter 11

Sarah ran along with the crowd, Drake following close behind. They were on the street called Blue Jay Way, running around car after car and hundreds of people as they all left the stadium simultaneously. She stopped at a wider street called Spadina, turned, and headed north, walking away from the lake.

She was free. Rod had been left behind. The bracelet had been removed, and there was nothing he could do about it now.

"How did you know who I was?" Sarah asked.

Drake caught up and walked beside her. "I saw your picture on the newspaper's front page two weeks ago. I remembered thinking how I'd love to meet you one day. It was very brave what you did."

They approached a red light. "Do you expect me to believe that?"

"It's the truth."

"So you saw a picture of me, and two weeks later, you

see me at a ball game, and that's it. Here we are."

"Yeah, that's what I expect you to believe because that's how it happened. Wait, why are you here?"

The light changed to green, and they continued north over Front Street and then up to King Street.

"I came to save your life," Sarah said.

"My life? Why? How did you know I needed saving?"

"It's a long story."

"Tell me. I have time."

Sarah looked at him. "Maybe one day."

She surprised herself at how she felt. Drake was gorgeous if that was possible for a man. Even for a man with almost no hair. It was like he was bald recently and was letting it grow back in. He seemed strong, witty, and brave, but she had no time to be interested in men. Someone had tried to shoot him thirty minutes ago, and he wasn't crying like a baby. She respected that.

"I see a fire in your eyes," Drake said.

"What?" Sarah turned to look the other way. Compliments sucked because they made everything awkward.

"Fire in your eyes. Your hair is stunning. Sarah, I remembered your face because it's rare for a man to see someone as beautiful as you."

"Drake, stop. Don't give me any pick-up lines. I'm warning you, this could turn out bad. You are only looking at me—you're not seeing the real me. I'm dangerous. People have a habit of dying around me, or I end up having to kill them."

He remained silent for a few steps, then said, "It's an honor to know you, Sarah, but you don't know anything about me, either. I just survived a grueling experience. An ex-girlfriend from high school, who I thought I would marry one day, tried to kill me, so I'm not afraid of your warning. I know it sounds corny, and we just met, but I feel I've known you for a long time, and since you just saved my life, I'm indebted to you, or at least until I can save your life one day."

Sarah snuck a glance at him. "Great. Look, I don't want to sound unappreciative, but who writes your material?"

It was out before she could take it back. A part of her had no problem with such a hot guy hanging around and attempting to save her life, but the truth was, her way of life was too risky for others. Her stomach twitched, but not from fear or nervousness. It came from a place of anticipation, one borne of being a woman and feeling desired.

What the fuck are you thinking? You've never had a boyfriend. You don't want one of those things. Fight it.

She looked at Drake and studied his jaw, perfect nose, and stunning eyes. Everything about him melted her. Even his deep voice caused her to shiver.

Shit. What the hell is happening to me? This is stupid.

She saw what looked like a coffee shop on the other side of the street. She guided him to the left, where they crossed Spadina and turned to cross Adelaide.

"What happened back there?" Drake asked. "How did you know they would try to kill me?"

"You were marked for death because of what happened to you recently, which I don't have a lot of details on."

"How come you're here and not a bunch of cops?"

She looked up at his gorgeous eyes. "I don't know. My sister has a sense of humor, maybe? Is this place a good one for coffee?"

Drake smiled. "Absolutely. Tim Horton's is the best. Come on."

Before going in, Sarah scanned the street behind them. Nothing odd or out of place. No one followed them, as far as she could tell.

A moment later, she stepped in behind Drake in line. After ordering two coffees, they took a table near the back, Sarah facing the front to watch the door.

Drake asked why she was in Toronto.

"There's not a lot to tell you," Sarah said. "I'm an automatic writer. My sister works through me to author notes about the future. My sister passed away shortly after I was born. Here, I'll show you what she told me an hour ago." Sarah grabbed the note about Drake's seat number and handed it to him, leaving the rest of the blank papers on the little table between them. "I know how it sounds, but it's the truth. I don't try to convince people anymore. Believe it or not, I don't really care."

"Wow, I've never heard of this kind of thing before. I mean, I know there are psychics and stuff, but this is actually real."

She could tell Drake was taken aback. Attempting to avoid direct contact with his eyes for fear of being swept away, Sarah told him about herself, some of what had recently happened in Europe, and why she had gotten Drake away from Spencer.

"So you think Spencer was in on this somehow?" Drake asked.

"I didn't say that. The note told me to beware of the cop and that he wanted to kill me. Spencer took you to the game where you were supposed to be killed. To be cautious, I thought we needed to be alone." She stopped and looked at him. "What I mean is …"

"I know what you mean," Drake said.

There's that fucking smile again. I feel like butter in the sun. It's nice, but it fucking sucks, too.

Drake went on for a few minutes, explaining what had happened to him two weeks ago and what some girl named Monika and her brothers had done to him. Drake had barely survived, but with quick thinking and a lot of luck, he had gotten through his ordeal with a shaved head and cast on his arm as his reward. Her respect for him went up tenfold.

She sipped at her coffee and watched the door, but no one who came or left paid them any extra attention.

Rod must be super pissed. Sarah grinned at the thought. *Fuck him. I'm sitting with a real man.*

"Innocent people died," Drake said. "Monika and her brother Attila were killed. Their father wants revenge. As far as I know, that's what today was all about. And all this because of falsified immigration documents."

"I've had my share of dealing with immigration fraud. I'm sick of it. We need to do something because this has to stop. You can't live under this threat."

What am I saying? Do we have to do something about this? Since when is it we? *Get it together, Sarah, there can be* no we.

Her hand twitched and went numb.

"Oh shit," Sarah said. "This is embarrassing. I'm about to blackout—"

She opened her eyes and lifted her head off the wall. She had slumped sideways, saving herself from the all-embarrassing kiss-the-floor routine.

Concern clouded his face.

He actually cares. Shit, I need a man in my life like I need a scorpion in my panties.

"You wrote something," Drake said. "What is it?"

Sarah looked at the paper in her hand and read the one word she had written in capital letters.

RUN!

Chapter 12

Sarah grabbed Drake's good arm and stood.

"You're coming with me," she said.

"Great." He smiled. The look of concern from a moment ago had disappeared.

"No jokes. This is serious."

"Whatever you say."

She walked through the opening in the counter and stepped into the back of the coffee shop, Drake in tow. Two men worked by a donut fryer.

"Is Mike here yet?" Sarah asked.

The bigger man of the two held a tray of uncooked donuts about to go into the fryer. "Who's Mike? We got no Mike works here."

"I'm Janet Reeds, and this is Kevin Miles," Sarah said. "We're from corporate. Mike is meeting us here to discuss the franchisee license infractions and complaints we have received. If he's not here yet, then we'll wait in our car in the back."

She stepped past the steel table in the middle and headed for the back door. No one said anything more or tried to stop them.

Confidence wins any time.

At the back door, Sarah heard a commotion coming from the front. Whoever they were running from had entered the coffee shop and was coming now.

Damn, that's fast.

She smacked the door hard, swung it open, and ran up the alley toward the next street.

"Come on," Sarah said as she pulled on Drake's shoulder. "We have to run."

"What's going on?"

"I have no idea, but when my sister says run, we run."

Cars raced by the entrance to the alley, all of them going to the left. The sign on her right said that Adelaide Street was a one-way. An orange taxi approached.

"Come on," Sarah said and ran toward it.

The cab driver noticed them and slowed, pulling to the side of the road. Sarah got in on one side and Drake on the other.

"Go!" Sarah said.

The driver hit the gas. Two seconds later, they passed the alley they'd just exited.

She saw Rod Howley running up to the street.

"Shit," Sarah said, slapping her hand on the door handle. "How did he find me so fast?"

"Who is that? And why is he looking for you?"

"I'll tell you later," Sarah said. Then leaned forward and addressed the driver. "Take us to the CN Tower."

The driver nodded, and Sarah sat back in her seat.

"Why the CN Tower?" Drake asked. "Do you realize how close that is to the baseball stadium? We just left that area."

"I know."

"Are you sure you want to go there?" Drake asked.

"They'd never expect us to head back that way."

Sarah took a few minutes in the cab's back seat to explain who Rod was and what he wanted from her. Drake became visibly upset the more she told him.

"How dare he? How's that even possible? Could one man be so powerful? That's dangerous in itself."

Sarah nodded and twisted in her seat to look out the back window. None of Rod's vehicles trailed them. Maybe this time, she had gotten away clean.

"Well, fuck him," Drake continued. "I'm sick of people pushing others around. It's time to push back and see how they dance."

Sarah raised her eyebrows, surprised by Drake's response but also liking it.

Drake saw her expression. "I'm serious," he said. "No more. I've been doing the right thing my whole life, trying to be socially correct. What did it get me? Attacked by a woman I once loved." He lowered his voice and leaned in close to Sarah. "People were murdered. I was almost killed numerous times. I'll have mental and physical scars forever. No more. Shit, I was almost shot again today."

The look in his eyes got her. Sarah actually felt lightheaded, which surprised her. She turned away from him and looked out the cab's window to hide her face. No one had ever spoken to her as deeply and as seriously as Drake did. A myriad of possibilities raced through her mind. Could

Drake be the one?

Too soon.

What was love like? After all she'd been through and done, all the people she'd killed or seen killed, was she capable of love? Or even allowed to love?

God willing.

Chapter 13

ELMORE PARKED HIS VEHICLE in an underground facility one block from the Rogers Centre. He had to act fast as the window of opportunity was closing. He locked his car, took the stairs two at a time, and walked along Front Street.

At the first bar he found, Elmore stepped inside and headed to the counter with all the confidence of a lead detective.

The woman behind the bar nodded.

"What'll it be?" she asked.

"I'm looking for this girl," Elmore said, holding out a picture of Sarah. "She escaped us at the Rogers Centre a few hours ago, and we're canvassing the area."

"You got ID?"

Elmore pulled out his fake detective badge and showed the woman. He felt like making her eat the ID but maintained resolve in his attempt to have Sarah.

"Haven't seen her," the woman said.

Bitch.

"You're late," she added.

"Late? How's that?" Elmore asked.

"Your colleagues were here an hour ago," the bartender said as she walked away.

Elmore left the bar, his spirits buoyed. If the cops were still in the area looking for Sarah, that meant she hadn't been picked up yet. She could be around the next corner.

He picked up his step and hit business after business along Front Street. He worked Bremner Boulevard and York Street until finally, two hours after the stampede at the Rogers Centre went live on Twitter, he turned up Spadina, where he headed north. With no luck, his mood soured.

His suit jacket covered the police uniform, and the fake mustache he had applied in the car was as thick as Magnum P.I.'s. He felt quite confident he'd never be placed in the vicinity as people wouldn't think to finger a detective when Sarah's missing persons case went into full gear.

All he needed was someone who had seen her enter a building or take a subway. Someone, anyone, to give him direction, and then he'd be on his way. Or if the police had her, at least he'd know.

The area quieted down as evening approached. The baseball fans had already left, except for the few stragglers who stayed behind to drink. Even the police presence had grown lighter.

"Shit, I was so close," he mumbled as he passed Adelaide Street.

He looked up at the Tim Horton's and decided to go in. Out of options, he walked up to the till in the nearly empty coffee shop and ordered a large black coffee.

The young girl behind the counter smiled at him and

turned to pour it for him. As a last resort, he pulled Sarah's picture out and set it on the counter.

The clerk turned back and set the coffee down beside the picture.

"Have you seen this girl today?" Elmore asked in his official cop voice.

The girl smiled at him. "Have I seen her? I'm the one who saw everything."

"Everything?" Elmore asked, instantly realizing he was just given another chance. "What does that mean?"

The girl looked around, her gaze stopping on the two customers in the store. Neither one paid them any attention. She turned back to Elmore.

"I work the three to eleven shift. Just before my shift, I was in the back office getting my cigarettes for a quick puff before my shift started. Two people came into the back and asked for some guy named Mike. Something about complaints from corporate." She waved her hand in the air. "There's no Mike here, so we brushed it off."

The girl leaned in closer to Elmore and whispered. "This girl in the picture and the guy she was with ran out the back and disappeared. I went to leave out the front door to have my cigarette and walked past a man with, like, four guys in tow. He looked seriously pissed. He also had a photo, and Louise told them the girl they were looking for just ran out the back."

"Wow," Elmore said to egg her on. "That's quite a story."

"But that's not the best part."

"It isn't?"

The girl shook her head hard, hair tossing about. "Nope. I ran up to the corner on Adelaide and, at the last second, saw the girl and the guy getting into a Beck cab. The taxi raced across Spadina and was lost to traffic as the angry guy stood at the end of the alley, still looking for her. When I saw him turn around and disappear back into the alley, I thought he was heading to Timmy's again, so I walked back to tell him what I saw."

"Did you end up telling this angry man what you saw?" Elmore asked, barely able to contain himself.

"No. When I walked back into the shop here, that angry man and his four goons weren't there. You're the first person I've told. No one else asked me shit."

Elmore could tell she was pleased with herself. The girl looked young and naïve. He wondered how much excitement she got out of life. He almost accidentally handed her his photo studio card to invite her to do a few pics. He would have blown his cop cover if he did.

Who was the guy Sarah was with?

"Thank you for your help. Someone will be in touch if we need more."

Elmore turned away and headed for the door.

"Hey, Mister, what about your coffee?"

Elmore didn't look back.

Chapter 14

DRAKE COULDN'T BELIEVE HE was on the run again. Just two weeks ago, killers had hunted him. Now it was cops. Or worse than cops. Rod Howley.

How could any government allow one man to possess so much power?

The other thing he couldn't wrap his head around was that he was on the run with Sarah Roberts.

How the hell did that happen?

Whatever divine fate brought them together, he planned to do whatever he could to keep them together. He was astounded at how beautiful she was. Her confidence, strength, and quick thinking grabbed him from the start. He'd been single too long. Sarah was exactly the kind of woman he could see himself spending a lot of time with.

If only they could get rid of all the people trying to kill them.

After they left the cab, they entered the CN Tower and lined up to purchase tickets to the top. Not being on the street would allow the heat to die down.

No way would that guy Rod find us up in the tower.

After getting their tickets, they entered another line for the elevator. It wasn't as long and moved well. Once inside the lift, he watched Toronto fall below their feet as the elevator rode the side of the building. A glass wall offered a stunning view as they climbed.

Drake cracked his jaw to pop his ears as they ascended.

"Sarah?" he whispered, leaning close to her. "How did you get that bruise on your wrist?"

She turned toward him. "Rod was keeping me prisoner. He used handcuffs when he kidnapped me off the plane and then placed a tracking device on my wrist for today's outing. I snapped it off five minutes before meeting you."

The elevator slowed to a stop. When the door opened and everyone exited, Drake led Sarah out to the circular windows, and the two of them looked at Toronto far below. The height was incredible.

After a walk around the circular tower, Drake led her to the glass floor. He stepped onto it and waited for Sarah to join him.

"I'm not going out there," she said.

"What? Are you serious? It's only about three hundred and fifty meters off the ground. The laminated glass is almost three inches thick. You'll be completely safe."

"No, I don't think so."

He could tell she wanted to, but some people hated that kind of thing.

"Come on, Sarah. I got you. I'll hold you."

Drake reached out to her. People came and went around them, minding their own business. One woman a few feet from Sarah also refused her husband's plea.

Drake lowered his head and stared at Sarah with yearning. It would give him a chance to touch her, to hold her. But it was too quick. They had just met. But Sarah exuded a power that drew him in like nothing he'd ever felt.

He moved his fingers to gesture one more time, and Sarah surprised him by stepping onto the glass. He wrapped her in his arms and held her tight, his cast resting on her shoulder. He felt her respond and let him hold her even as she shuddered when she looked down.

"Why the hell would anyone step out onto a piece of flimsy glass this high up?" Sarah asked. "Whoever thought of this had to be insane. What would the epitaph read? Lived a full life, stepped on glass, and fell to her death. Fucking idiot. You know, Drake, I'm not afraid of heights … it's the fall that sucks."

Drake's cell phone rang.

Sarah stepped out of his arms and off the glass. "I'm good for now," she said and stayed off to the side as Drake pulled his phone out to see who it was.

Spencer.

"Hello?"

"Where are you?" Spencer asked.

"Looks like we may have a problem."

"Of course we do." Spencer sounded pissed. "It's not over. We couldn't locate the shooter. Tell me where you are so I can come and pick you up and get you under police protection."

"Right. So you can lead the shooter to me? Not a chance."

"What are you talking about? Lead the shooter to you?"

"Spencer, I know you were there at the end of two weeks ago. I know you stopped Monika, but what happened at the ball game today happened because you took me there."

Drake moved to the corner to avoid anyone hearing his end of the conversation.

"You're talking crazy. I'm still at the Rogers Centre. We're trying to piece this thing together. American officials are here. That girl you ran away with is an international criminal and wanted by every agency they have down there, including the FBI."

Drake snuck a glance at Sarah while he listened. She smiled back.

"If you can't talk," Spencer continued, "no problem, listen. Find a way to tell me where you are. I'll bring everything I have, and we'll stop her together. She's wanted on charges of killing her ex-boyfriend with a knife to the stomach. They only brought her here from Chicago this afternoon to help them identify someone. How you got mixed up with her, no one knows. Help me bring her in, Drake."

Drake gripped the phone tighter. He recalled something Sarah had said. *I'm dangerous. People have a habit of dying around me, or I have to kill them.* What did that really mean? Who was she, and could any of what Spencer said be true?

He couldn't hear anymore. He had to figure things out on his own. But who could he trust?

"Beware of a half-truth. You may have the wrong half," Drake said and closed his phone without saying goodbye.

"What was that all about?" Sarah asked.

"It was Spencer. The cop that took me to the ball game."

He felt her eyes on him, studying, scrutinizing. "Then why the long face?" she asked. "What did he say?"

Drake looked at her and wasn't sure what he saw anymore: a traitor or his savior. "I just can't believe I was had so easily. I hate being lied to. I'm finished with toxic people."

Sarah nodded and stepped out into the hallway. Drake followed as she led him toward the elevators.

"It's time to go," Sarah said. "We need to get underground, find a cheap motel to discuss what to do next. I need to locate Parkman somehow. He'll be able to help."

"Who's Parkman?"

"He's a good friend and a cop. I'll explain more later."

Drake didn't feel like talking anymore.

The line wrapped around away from the elevator. After a ten-minute wait, they'd moved far enough to be able to see the elevator doors. The tension thickened between them. Drake didn't know what to believe. Should he ask her about the death of her ex-boyfriend? How would she take it? In the end, he figured she'd deny it.

Yeah, Drake, sorry, I had to kill that guy. He was a terrible boyfriend.

The elevator arrived. As it emptied, the people in line ahead of them began to enter.

The last five people off the elevator all wore the same jackets. Drake noticed them right away. They scanned faces, dodged people, and attempted to get somewhere fast. Sarah ducked her head and leaned into the wall, moving toward the elevator.

"That's Rod," Sarah whispered to him. "How the fuck did he find us so fast?"

It was time to solve everything. If Sarah did hurt or kill someone, and they are looking for her, then I have to do the right thing. If she's done nothing wrong, then what could it hurt?

He wondered how Rod's tracking skills could be so good. Something unexplainable was happening here. Rod was never too far behind.

And what was that about Sarah wearing a tracking device and handcuffs? Could he really be on the run with a criminal? They didn't use cuffs and tracking devices on innocent people.

If Sarah was guilty of something, then as much as he was attracted to her and would love to get to know her better, he couldn't help her.

With his mind made up, Drake stepped out of line and walked away from Sarah.

"Rod Howley," he shouted. "Sarah and I are right here."

Rod turned from about twenty feet away and stared as he pointed toward where Sarah stood near the elevator's door.

Chapter 15

ELMORE RAN FROM THE Tim Horton's, and on his way back to his car, he dialed Beck Taxi's dispatch.

"Beck Taxi?"

"My name is Staff Sergeant Mike King. I'm interested in a fare that got picked up near the corner of Adelaide and Spadina just over an hour ago. It was a young couple. According to the information we've received, the cab was flagged down. It wasn't called in."

"I'm sorry, who are you?" the dispatcher asked.

"Mike King. I'm the lead detective investigating the shooting at the Rogers Centre. We have reason to believe the person of interest took one of your cabs."

"Look, sir, I can't give you that kind of information over the phone."

He ran through traffic at the red light on King Street and continued toward his car, trying to formulate his response. He had to find out where Sarah was dropped off to get there before anyone else could.

"Ma'am, I know you're aware of the Freedom of Information Act. I could go to any judge in the city and get him to sign a warrant to read your dispatch logs. The difference is that it would take until tomorrow or the day after to get the information, and that would be a problem."

He stopped talking to let the dispatcher respond. When she didn't, Elmore continued, "If you tell me what I need to know now, you save us both a lot of trouble and time. While you decide, remember that we're hunting a killer on the streets of Toronto. Do you really want that on your conscience if they kill again when you could've done something to stop it?"

He heard no response. With all the traffic going by, Elmore wasn't sure if he'd been disconnected.

Then the dispatcher spoke.

"I've only been here a few months. I don't want to lose my job. I can't do it."

"Okay then, I'll tell you what. Give me what I need, and I will personally talk to your boss or whoever you want and tell them that the Toronto police force is indebted to you for your service to the community. I will make their life hell if they even think of firing you. But, on the other hand, go by the book on this one and make me get a warrant. I will tell your boss how difficult you were to work with regarding the location of a murder suspect. I will formally recommend you are fired immediately. Work with me, and I will work for you. That's how this goes. Get it?"

Elmore had made it to the building where his car sat parked underground. He had to wait until the call ended before heading down, or he'd lose the signal.

"We're running out of time here," Elmore prodded.

"Make a choice but make the right one. Help me catch a murderer, and I will help you. Decision time."

Another pause made him feel the dispatcher was going to disappoint him.

"The CN Tower," she said.

"What? Really?"

"Yeah, I got it right here."

Elmore slammed his phone shut and ran down the ramp for his car. The CN Tower sat only one city block away from him. He could be there in less than four minutes.

He jumped in his car and squealed the tires a few times as he raced out of the parking lot.

When he hit Front Street, he set his red police light on the vehicle's dash and turned it on. As they do in the movies, he jammed on his brakes in front of the tower, opened his door, got out, and slammed it shut.

His exposure was high, but with the fake mustache, the clothing, and the proper ID, Elmore was confident he could pull it off.

He ran through the main doors, showed his badge, and headed for the elevators, where he stopped.

A group of seven men stood in a circle around one elevator door, guns drawn, all watching, waiting as the lift rode down its cables from the top.

Sarah, I got you.

Chapter 16

SARAH HAD SEEN ROD. She whispered to Drake and started for the open door of the elevator, ducking down to avoid detection.

Drake had stepped out of line and called Rod's name.

What the fuck is he doing?

Sarah looked across the corridor and into the eyes of Rod Howley. He bolted into action, running at her, his face showing all his anger in an instant.

Sarah grabbed Drake's arm, yanking once.

"Let's go!" she shouted and pulled him toward the open elevator. There were too many people. The door crowded up as everyone tried to gain access to the lift.

A glance over her shoulder confirmed Rod was five feet away.

"Gun!" she shouted in the most hysterical voice she could summon. "He's got a gun. Everybody, run!"

She expected instant chaos, but only a few people reacted, looking around to see who carried a weapon.

What is it with the people of Toronto? Does everyone have a gun?

She had succeeded in clearing the doors enough, but Drake had trouble. Rod was right behind him, reaching for Drake.

"Shoot him," Sarah yelled. "Use your gun. Kill the scum where he stands."

That got people moving faster. Rod had caused a scene by running at Drake and Sarah. Men and women ran away from the elevator. One woman shouted that she was calling the police. Another woman just screamed.

Sarah lowered her center of gravity and grabbed Drake around the waist. She pulled him into the elevator while three people edged past them on their way out.

The door began to shut. It got caught and opened again.

Sarah moved to the right and jammed her thumb on the close door button, holding it down.

"Drake, get that fucking door clear," she yelled at him.

Whatever he heard in her voice, Drake complied. He pushed forward like a defensive linebacker, holding his cast up as he pushed, clearing the door far enough for it to close.

Just before the door closed completely, Sarah saw Rod's face in the small gap of inches. His expression was complete and utter hatred for having to deal with her this way.

It must really fuck him up to always be chasing me.

Then she turned to Drake. There were three other men still on the elevator with them. All three moved away from her as she glared at Drake.

She brought her hands up, grabbed his collar, and shoved him up against the wall.

"What the fuck were you thinking?"

One of the men on the elevator touched her shoulder. "Hey, take it easy. It's over. Let him go."

Sarah slapped the hand off her shoulder. "Whatever touches me again gets broken. Don't test me when I'm this pissed off."

She looked into Drake's eyes, nose to nose. "What was that all about?"

"Get off me," Drake said. "We will talk when you're not in my face."

Sarah let him go and looked out the glass wall at Toronto, rising to meet them.

"Is it true?" Drake asked. "Did you really knife your ex-boyfriend in the stomach, and you're wanted for murder?"

She eyed him for a moment. "Spencer tell you that?"

Drake nodded.

"Believe what you want," Sarah said as she stepped to the corner of the elevator.

"No." Drake shook his head. "I want to hear it from you. Are you the hero I thought you were, or a criminal on the run?"

Tears of disappointment edged into her eyes. "I will tell you this. I'm no hero."

She couldn't believe she had actually started to feel something for Drake. Sure he was hot, but she could do without the drama. If he was that easy to sway, anyone could tell him anything, and he'd play for that team. Rod had almost got her again.

Rod would radio down to have cops waiting at the bottom. There had to be a way out. The roof was too high to try the square access door. The only way out was the main door.

She looked through the glass, and Toronto disappeared as the elevator entered the building at the base and slowed.

She was out of time.

"Okay, you three, upfront. Watch the doors."

The three strangers did what they were told. After hearing talk of murder, she was sure none of them really wanted to test her.

"What are you doing?" Drake asked.

She definitely heard hurt feelings in his voice.

Yeah, well, I'm hurt, too.

"Rod will have called down. People will be waiting for us. There's no way I'm going back with him to his bunker."

The elevator came to a complete stop. All five of them looked forward as the doors started to open.

Hunkering down low, with no sight of what lay beyond the doors, Sarah could feel the police presence.

No one on the elevator moved.

She glanced over the shoulder of the guy who had touched her a few moments ago.

More than half a dozen cops stood in a semicircle, their weapons aimed at the inside of the elevator.

It's over. Rod has gotten me again. Fuck, how could he track me so well?

The lights on the elevator turned off. The power went out.

"Nobody fucking move," Sarah said. "I'm serious."

"Sarah Roberts, please step out of the elevator," a voice commanded from beyond. "It has been taken out of service. The doors will not close. You have nowhere to go. Come out with your hands up."

Chapter 17

ELMORE RAN UP TO the back of the line of cops as the elevator doors opened.

He flashed his badge and turned to a cop beside him.

"I'm to take Sarah Roberts and her companion into my custody. I'm with the Americans. She's to wait in my vehicle out front until they can rendezvous with me here."

The privately hired armed security guards surrounding the elevator looked nervous. The one Elmore spoke to seemed eager to have Sarah off his radar.

"Sure, if you can get her off that elevator. We're not going in there."

Elmore edged between two guards and stepped to the elevator door.

"Okay, let's go," Elmore said. "You three, get off the elevator first."

The three in the front hustled out and away from the door. He was running out of time. At any second, real authorities would show up. He would be arrested. He had to get her now and do it fast.

He stepped to the open door and saw her silhouette in the darkened elevator. A feeling of major achievement washed over him. Sarah Roberts, the real Sarah Roberts, was all his, to do what he pleased for as long as he wanted.

"Sarah, you're to come with me," he said. He knew how much that cop Parkman worked with her. He leaned his head in farther and whispered, "Parkman sent me. I'll take you to him, but you must hurry."

She stepped from the shadows. He couldn't believe it. He had her. His Sarah. Oh, she would be a delight to kiss, to suck on. It would be an honor to use her nails between his teeth. Her panties would sell so well.

He stepped from the lift and nodded at the guards who lowered their weapons.

"I got this. They will come with me to my vehicle out front and wait there. You," Elmore pointed at the man he spoke to earlier, "will you help escort these two prisoners to my vehicle?"

The man nodded. "The show's over," he announced to the gathering crowd.

Elmore wrapped his hand around Sarah's arm and instantly began growing an erection. He led her away as the rent-a-cop grabbed the other guy and followed.

He couldn't believe how easy it was.

He also couldn't believe that just holding onto Sarah's arm aroused him this much.

Oh, Sarah, we will have a lot of fun together.

The foursome made it out of the building without being stopped. He chanced a look behind him, but no one had given chase yet. It wouldn't be long. The people hunting Sarah were close. They had almost had her. His timing couldn't have been more perfect.

They reached his car. He opened the door, and the guy Sarah was with got in, followed by Sarah. As soon as the door closed, they were his. The doors were locked on the outside like a regular police car. There was no way either one of them could get out unless he let them out.

He could never tell when an unwilling female hostage would change her mind on the way to his house and decide to jump from his vehicle. That kind of attention would be undesirable.

"Thanks for your help," Elmore said to the guard. He slapped him on the shoulder and said, "Tell them I'm out here when they come for her."

"Okay," the guard said and started back for the tower.

Elmore ran around to the driver's seat and got in. He fired up the engine and flicked on the headlights as the evening had dropped into dusk.

He put the car in gear and started away. The flashing light on his dash bothered him. He unplugged it from his cigarette lighter and tossed it on the passenger side floor.

Then he looked in the mirror and laughed.

I've actually got Sarah Roberts in my car, and no one knows me, or where we're going, he thought. *Both of you are now missing persons cases that'll never be found.*

Chapter 18

THE SIGN ON THE side of the road said they were on the Gardiner Expressway. As far as Sarah could tell, the driver wasn't heading to the island airport. That meant they weren't flying out, and he probably wasn't with Parkman.

But how did he know to use Parkman's name?

She tapped on the Plexiglas. "Where are we going?"

She caught the driver's eyes in the mirror, looking at her. He didn't respond.

Something was wrong again. Why did she always get herself caught up in shit? Couldn't something go right for a change? Parkman would have come himself. She wouldn't just trust anybody. Yet, she did. So why did she go with this man? Because it was a way out of the elevator situation.

She turned to Drake.

This was all his fault.

Drake turned to her, his face showing concern.

She pointed at the driver with her hand held low and shook her head. Then she mouthed the word, problem.

He nodded and pulled out his cell phone. Drake dialed a number and waited for it to connect.

Vivian had warned her. Beware the cop. He's fake. He wants to kill you.

Could the driver be the fake cop Vivian referred to? It had to be.

Drake said, "Spencer? Sorry for hanging up earlier."

Whether the fake cop Vivian referred to as Spencer or the driver of the car, attempting to get help from Spencer would reveal which one it was. She had to let things play out to decide who to hurt when the shit went down.

"I don't know what's going on," Drake continued. "The Americans chased us out of the CN Tower, and now we're in a cop car heading along the Gardiner—"

The driver slammed on the brakes so hard that both of them shot forward into the Plexiglas. Sarah had just enough time to save her face by getting her hands up. Drake only got his right up in time as his left was holding the phone to his ear. Neither had put on seat belts.

"Motherfucker," Drake shouted.

Sarah's heart opened a little more for him. *My kind of man.*

"Throw your phone out the window," the driver said as he resumed his speed on the highway.

The window on Drake's side slid down an inch.

"Do it now."

Drake looked at Sarah and then at his phone. Then he addressed the driver. "Fuck you," he said. "You gonna buy me a new one, asshole." Then he put the phone back to his ear. "Spencer? You still there?"

The driver tapped his brakes a couple of more times.

"Do it now or pay a severe price."

"Hey, asshole. I don't know who you are, but I've been through a tough two weeks. Whether you really are a cop or not, I don't give a shit about you. What I do care about is my phone. So fuck off."

Sarah hadn't met a man in a long time who looked as good as Drake and talked so seductively. He had potential. Maybe there'd be a day when they could spend some quality time together.

But I'd have to trust him. What he did in the CN Tower was fucked.

The car jerked to the right. As fast as they got on the highway, they were exiting. The driver acted like a madman. He plugged his police light in again, the red orb flashing on his dash. At the bottom of the ramp, he turned a hard right and then a left into a gas station parking lot.

It was all they could do to stay seated in the upright position.

The driver stopped the vehicle, got out, and ran around the car to Drake's side.

"Get ready. Here's our chance," Sarah said.

Drake turned in his seat and brought his feet up at the door. Sarah braced herself and got ready.

The door lock clicked, and the door opened. Drake thrust with his feet but met empty air. The driver's head peeked in. He had something in his hand.

She closed her eyes almost instantly at the hissing sound.

Drake shouted. In the confined space of the back seat, his voice sounded deafening.

She couldn't breathe without taking a little in.

Pepper spray.

She had to keep her eyes closed but knowing what was happening made her open them a slit.

Drake hacked and coughed. His face was red, and his eyes were running.

She tried to open her door, but it was locked from the outside. Drake's door slammed shut. The driver got back in and drove away from the gas station, his police light turned off now. In moments, they were on the elevated highway again.

She could open her eyes a little more, but she breathed through the collar of her shirt. Drake rubbed his eyes and moaned. His phone was nowhere in sight.

Breathing became more difficult. It looked like Drake was losing his battle.

She banged on the Plexiglas.

"He's dying back here. We need air, or I'm going to die, too."

Or is that what you want? Fuck, how do I always get myself mixed up with the worst assholes on the planet?

Both windows slid down an inch. In unison, Drake and Sarah put their noses as close to the fresh air as they could. Her nose cleared almost instantly, but she could hear Drake's breathing still labored. She could only imagine the pain he was going through.

She knew the price of bravado, but sometimes there was nothing left in life but standing up for yourself and what you believe in at all costs.

"Defy me again," the driver said. "And the price goes up each and every time."

Fear crept over her like a cloak.

Who is this guy? Where is he taking us?

Oh, Vivian, I'm sorry, I know you warned me, but I need your help here ...

115

<h1 style="text-align:center">Chapter 19</h1>

Elmore drove the most direct route north of Toronto to Highway 27 and up to Nobleton. He turned up his driveway and meandered along the winding lane. No one bothered him in his fortified house secluded behind a thick forest.

How much luck could one man have?

Just that morning, he'd removed Jackie from her cage because Sarah Roberts was probably coming back to North America soon. That afternoon she was seen in Toronto, and now she was captive in the back seat of his car. He couldn't believe it. He'd finally got her. A five-year obsession concluded.

He parked near the front door of his house. No one knew anything about him or where they were. If anyone caught a glimpse of his license plate number, it would never lead the police to him. The plate had been registered to an abandoned wreck parked two blocks from his studio in downtown Toronto for a month. Two days ago, the wreck was still there.

He smiled. The time had come. The time was his to

control. He had become the master, and Sarah Roberts was his slave.

Elmore got out and entered his house, leaving the two prisoners in his vehicle. He walked through the main floor, turned on lights, and went downstairs to set up the basement. After opening both cage doors, he grabbed two pairs of handcuffs and one of his 9mm semi-automatic Mamba pistols and made his way back out to the car.

The back windows were still down the inch he had allowed them for air, but the male looked worse. He needed to flush his eyes and get cleaned up.

Elmore placed the handcuffs at the crack in the window and let them both fall in.

"Place the handcuffs on, and I will open the door. Then we will go into the house and discuss what will happen here."

"Yeah, and I'll do a tap dance and flit around like Peter Pan," Sarah said. "How's that? You want to hear any more fairy tales, dick fuck?"

"I don't think you understand the gravity of your situation," Elmore said as he leaned closer to the open window. He grabbed the end of his fake mustache and slowly pulled it off. "You're mine now. There is no escape." He pulled his Mamba out and showed it to her. "These little guys run a lot faster than you." He put the gun back. "I know you're strong, Sarah. But this part is easy. Put the cuffs on and come on inside so we can discuss what to do next."

"Fuck you," she said and raised her middle finger.

Elmore shook his head. "Disappointed in you, Sarah. No one knows where you are. No one can hear you. No one in Toronto knows me. There is nothing you can do that'll alter your situation in any way. It's over, Sarah. Put the handcuffs on or stay in the car all night. Your choice."

She turned away from the window.

Fine. She'll learn who's tougher.

Elmore walked back into the house and entered his office. He booted up his computer and leaned back in his chair to wait. Once his news feeds had loaded, he scanned them diligently. Below his desk was the cell phone jammer, which he should've brought with him so he wouldn't have had to pull over and spray that guy's face.

He flicked it on in case Sarah had a cell phone. He never patted anyone down for electronics. Too dangerous when the girls first arrived. His Wi-Fi jammer worked perfectly.

He wondered why there was no news about Sarah's kidnapping or the man she was with. Sarah was a celebrity now. Why wouldn't the media have something about what happened at the CN Tower?

Maybe it was too soon. He'd keep an eye on it overnight.

Who is that guy with her?

He'd find out soon enough. In the coming days, he'd know everything about both of them. He would get to know Sarah on a more intimate level. She'd be a good lay. If she weren't compliant, he'd drug her food and do what he wanted with her unconscious form for hours while the male watched from the adjacent cell. He'd prefer Sarah awake. He loved it when he pumped between a woman's legs while she cried. He couldn't get an unconscious female to cry, so he'd have to keep her awake for some of their trysts. Maybe he would secure her to the point where she couldn't move any body part. That would work.

Making Sarah Roberts cry had been his dream for almost five years since he'd first heard about her exploits. He couldn't believe his time had finally come. He now possessed his very own Sarah Roberts.

Elmore opened the desk drawer and withdrew the fingernail container. He uncapped it, grabbed the thickest one, and placed it between his front teeth. Then he leaned back and started working on the scab.

This is life.

He smiled, staring at the collage of images on the wall across the room. "Oh, yeah," he said out loud. "Sarah Roberts will cry before I'm done with her. We are going to have such a good time together, Sarah. You'll see. You'll come to enjoy me, too. It only takes time, Sarah. I know you'll grow to love me as I love you."

Chapter 20

After the fake cop disappeared into the house, Sarah redoubled her efforts on the door. She turned in the seat and laid her back down so she could kick at the glass. Nothing worked.

Drake breathed harder still. He got progressively worse without the aid of fresh air rushing through the windows.

Oh, Parkman, where are you? I could really use your help here.

She grabbed the door handle and continued her attack.

"It ith no uth," Drake said. "Here." He handed her one pair of the cuffs. "I need wather."

She understood. They were out of options. They had to change their circumstances. It would allow her to find a different way out. Nothing worked stuck in the car.

She gently placed the cuffs onto her bruised wrists but kept them bound in front of her.

They waited, silently hoping the man would come back soon. After an hour, the house's front door opened, and the driver started down the front steps to make his way to the car.

Sarah held up her cuffs to show him. He nodded and smiled and looked for Drake's. He also held them up.

"Okay, good," the man said. "Now, add one more click so I know they're secure and not on too loose, and then we'll go inside."

Sarah clicked hers, and Drake clicked his. Every second they were in the driver's presence, Sarah felt anger mixed with fear. He was too cool, too calm. One word resounded in her head: dangerous.

"Okay," the man said. "Before I open the door, I have to warn you. Any act I deem aggressive toward my person or any attempt to escape will be met with more pepper spray—but I will empty the canister into your nose directly. When I drag you into the house, I will cut your body into as many pieces as I can and then make the other one of you eat the remains. Do not betray me. The stakes have been claimed, and the price is too high. Are we clear?"

They both nodded their heads.

The door clicked on Sarah's side. The man opened it and stepped back, a pistol in his hand.

What was that rant about pepper spray? Now it's a gun?

He motioned for them to walk ahead of him. The house sprawled before her. There was some kind of patio on the roof, but it was too dark to make anything out other than the railing.

She entered first into the house. It was so clean it almost looked sterilized. Off to the right of the main foyer sat large double doors that opened to a huge office. A banker's desk sat near the window.

"This way," the man motioned to the left with his gun

toward the basement door.

Halfway down, Sarah saw the large cages. She slowed her step and turned to see Drake right behind her. The driver raised his weapon and aimed it at her face.

"Keep moving. You're in the one on the right."

Sarah ran through her options but came up empty. Even if she grabbed something to throw, she wouldn't be that effective with her hands cuffed in front of her.

She stepped down to the concrete floor and walked up to the cage door. She had to do something. She couldn't willingly walk into a death chamber. But what? She had no weapon and no way to wield one.

"I know what you're thinking, but remember the consequences. The price is too high. Continue forward, or I'll shoot you in the leg and leave you alive long enough to do unspeakable things to you."

Reluctantly, Sarah stepped into the cage, wondering if she would ever see outside the basement again.

The man came up behind her and shut the door, securing it with some kind of electronic lock. There was a small toilet, a clock on the back wall, and a cot-sized mattress on the floor. A thin blanket lay spread over the mattress.

Drake entered his cell, equipped with the same interior. The walls were thick concrete all the way up to a concrete ceiling. The wall between the two cells consisted of half bars and half concrete. She could see Drake and his cot but not the back area where his toilet would be, nor could he see hers.

He'd done this before. These cages weren't just erected for her. In that case, could it be possible Vivian had allowed her to be taken so she'd locate this madman and be able to stop him?

He had an expert approach. The cages, the decked-out vehicle with a fake ID, and a police siren. The man was a professional. He had nerves of steel to pull off what he did to get them there.

She sized everything up. All the bad guys were the same; they just wore different clothes. It was always a different set of circumstances, but she would prevail. Vivian wouldn't have let her get trapped this easily. Something good would come her way.

The man stepped away from view and then, a moment later, came back with three water bottles in his hands. He tossed one through Sarah's bars and the other two through to Drake.

Drake fumbled around, grabbed one, tilted his head back, and poured it all over his face, using his free hand to rub the water in.

The man stepped into Sarah's cage and stared at her. His eyes roamed her body. She wanted to reach through the bars and tear them out of their sockets.

"I'll be back later to talk. I will explain everything soon enough. I'm sure you'll grow to enjoy your stay with me. Once you know my rules, things'll become easier." He stared into her eyes. "Sarah Roberts, you're my little hostage now."

He stepped away, ascended the stairs, and left the basement, turning off the light as he shut the door.

Chapter 21

Something burned Sarah's ankle. She rolled over and smacked at it with both hands. Then something hot touched her side by her hip bone. She got up and swatted at it. She idly wondered if she'd been stung by a bee.

Then she remembered where she was. A cage in a madman's basement. A burned-out match smoldered on the floor. Her tormentor had thrown lit matches at her.

"Wake up," he said. "It's five in the morning—time to wake up."

"You wake me up with fucking matches?"

The man hadn't uncuffed them yet as he didn't return last night. A single overhead light cast him in an eerie glow. Sarah could barely see Drake's feet at the edge of his little mattress. She couldn't tell if he was alive or dead.

"Don't worry about him. He's fine. We need to talk."

"About what?"

The man slipped a thin box through the bars of her cage's door and tossed it close to her. Then he leaned down and slid a small piece of something metallic along the floor.

"That's a nail clipper. No long nails are allowed in my cells. Clip your fingernails and then your toenails. Do not let them touch the floor. Once you've collected all of them, hand them to me and slide the clipper back out."

"Forget it. You aren't getting shit from me until you tell me what this is all about."

The man seemed to consider this for a moment.

"My name is Elmore. I operate an international company that sells used panties. In that box, you'll find a variety of panties in many colors. Over the course of the next few days, you will wear the panties for at least six hours a day and then place them back in the box after you've been photographed wearing them for authentication purposes. That's what this is all about."

Sarah couldn't believe what she was hearing. "Are you serious? Used panties? That's insane. Who would buy such a thing?" His expression didn't change. He wasn't joking. "You kidnapped me to make me wear panties for your company? Are you insane? What the fuck are you? Nobody does shit like that."

"You'll do as I say. I know you will because you're not my only hostage. He is, too." The man nodded toward Drake. "When you prove difficult, I will start to take body parts off him one by one and mix them in with his food. You can watch your friend eat himself alive over the coming months. I've got all the time in the world, as do you."

Sarah felt something akin to horror. "You are certifiably fucking gone. Those words you just said signed your death sentence. When I get out of here, I will murder you with these hands." She held them high for him to see.

Elmore stepped back from her bars. "You might want to monitor your threats, as I'm the one on this side of the cage. Clip your nails now. You don't have the option to say no. And don't worry; we'll get along in time. You'll grow to depend on me and love me."

"Fat fuck-off chance," she said. Then she mumbled, "The only thing I'll love about you is watching you die at the end of my arms, you sick fuck."

"I warned you about the threats."

Elmore moved away from her cell door and started toward Drake's.

"Wait."

He stopped.

"The tongue is better than a sharp knife. It kills without drawing blood," she said. She couldn't let anything happen to Drake on account of her attitude. "Sometimes, my words get away from me."

"Nails. Start clipping."

She got off the mattress and picked up the clipper. After doing her nails, she stepped over to the toilet, held them over it, and then flushed them down.

She turned around and smiled at him. "Sorry about that. This batch was a little dirty. I saw how clean your house is. You wouldn't want those nails." She shrugged, then added, "You'll have to wait a few weeks until they grow back out."

"You really don't get it, do you?" He walked under the light and crossed his arms. "I'm your everything now. All my girls break. You'll break, too. I've been looking forward to this for five years. You're not superhuman. I'm your only source of food, water, the outside world, and companionship. Maslow's hierarchy of needs is right here. I'm it."

"You're an entire hierarchy of asshole if you think you'll be able to break me. I'm the one looking forward to this because I will get out and when I do, the price will be too high for you. You won't be able to handle the cost."

Elmore blew air out of his mouth. "I expected you to be strong, but you're showing strength beyond your years. Admirable, Sarah, admirable. But I've been doing this for a long time. There have been a lot of young girls in those cages over those years, and all of them are buried out back after spending a few months servicing me and my needs, whether it was business needs or personal needs. You will be no different. And guess what?"

He stepped closer to her cell door. "Not a single cop ever came to my door looking for a lost girl. I'm too good. Are you even aware of how many people go missing every day and are never seen again? My basement is soundproof. No one saw you come here. You've disappeared. The next time you see the sun again will be when I take your used dead body upstairs to bury you out back. That's what's going on here."

She couldn't let him see how he was getting to her. She realized he was right. If no one knew where they were or where to look, she might be in his cell for some time.

Keep him talking. Find a hole somewhere.

"How could you be that good?" she asked. "No one can stay under the radar that long."

"I have. It's been so easy. The girls come to me. They're so stupid."

"How's that?" Keep him talking.

Elmore unfolded his arms and turned away from her. He grabbed a small armchair and carried it to the front of her cell, where he sat and leaned forward on his thighs.

"The panty business is legitimate. I own a photo studio in downtown Toronto. I have ads in local papers for non-nude photography, but no experience is necessary. Do you know how many responses I get for those ads? In the hundreds per week."

Sarah's stomach dropped. The man before her was the worst kind of predator. Brilliant, cunning, and dangerous. She couldn't detect an ounce of sympathy, care, or guilt in him. Females were simply on earth to provide a service to him, even if that service was sex.

"The real draw for these girls," he continued, "is that none of the pictures are ever of their face. I don't need that, only the panties. They whine and complain during the shoots. Their boyfriend is horrible, or their parents disowned them. They're living with friends. Things like that. But once every few weeks, a girl will enter my studio and tell me that nobody knows I'm here story. She couldn't tell anyone because they'd be upset. These girls are down on their life with nothing really going for them. So I offer them an amazing opportunity. I need someone at our bigger studio north of Toronto to do a glamour shoot, and they'd be perfect. I compliment them just enough. Sarah, you could almost see their eyes widen at their newfound luck."

She hated every time he used her name. She got down on the floor with no chair to sit on and crossed her legs.

"I even offer them a full-time job at ten thousand bucks a month. They usually fall for everything I spoon-feed them. When they've agreed, I offer to drive them up and show them the studio right away so they can meet the other executives. I drive them here, and all they meet is another girl that I've held captive for the past few months. The new girl gets to watch while I have the old one perform numerous sex acts on me, and then I kill her. Having the new girl see what's in store for her if she doesn't behave is quite something. A man has never had sex like the kind coming from an obedient eighteen-year-old doing exactly what she's told to do."

Sarah almost got up and ran to the bars. Knowing they were steel made no difference. At that moment, she would find a way through. It took everything in her power to contain all urges of murder.

She wanted to weep for all the young girls this beast of a man had hurt.

When he comes looking for something, I'll be waiting. He'll be dead soon.

"Sometimes I just need a change or meet a prettier girl at the studio." He shrugged and looked down at his hands. "The best, kinkiest sex comes from frightened girls. They do it thinking they'll keep me happy. If I'm happy, they rationalize, maybe I'll begin to like them, and it'll be different for them. I even let these stupid ones think things are going their way." He looked up at Sarah. His left hand went to his head, where he picked at something. "How pathetic are they? I only use them. The pleasure I take is in their pain. My existence is misery. I know who and what I am and am comfortable with it. I love it when I'm pumping them, and they're crying. There is no greater sex." He stood from his chair. "One day, I'll make you cry, too, Sarah. You watch."

She felt detached from the conversation. Like it wasn't happening. Somehow, it didn't feel real. The day he touched her would be when she drove her thumbs into his eye sockets to the back of his skull.

"Now, the price you have to pay for the fingernails in the toilet mistake will be one bullet in your friend here. Somewhere low so he won't bleed out too much."

Elmore stood and walked closer to Drake's cell door, his gun in his hand again.

"Wait. I'll get you the nails."

"Too late, Sarah. They're dirty now. I told you not to let them touch the floor. The toilet is a little worse. You understand who I am now, so you'll also know I don't play games."

Drake's feet moved. Either he'd been awake or was just waking up.

"Let's talk about this."

Shit. There's nothing I can do.

"The time for deal-making is over now."

Elmore lifted the weapon and took careful aim.

Something banged upstairs. Sarah turned at the same time Elmore did.

"What was that?" he asked out loud.

She detected doubt in his voice. Something was wrong above. That meant no one else was supposed to be in the house. Otherwise, the sound wouldn't have startled him so much.

The noise came again.

Knocking.

The asshole left the basement door open, and now someone's pounding on the front door.

"Feed an opportunity, starve a problem," Sarah said. "You fail."

Elmore's face changed instantly to anger. The gun

disappeared into the back of his pants as he ran for the stairs, taking them two at a time.

The single bulb flicked off, and the door slammed shut at the top of the stairs.

The lock clicked as Sarah tried to get her breathing back under control.

That was close. That was too fucking close.

Chapter 22

ELMORE LOCKED THE BASEMENT door and moved down the hallway quietly. It had to be six in the morning. Who could be at his door? Even door-to-door preachers stayed out of the area because it was too hard to walk the long distances between houses.

As much as he wanted to believe otherwise, he had no doubt that it was the police at his door. But how? He couldn't think of a single mistake he'd made. How could they track him so well? He'd been too good for too many years. It didn't make sense. He wasn't followed. His cell phone jammer covered radio frequency devices too, so it wasn't that.

In the living room, he pulled a curtain back. Two black and whites were parked out front. A couple of uniformed men stood by the vehicles, and two men stood at his door.

Cops. Fuck.

He slipped into his office, took the gun out of his pants, placed it in the bottom drawer of his desk, and then hustled back to the door.

When he had gotten up from his short sleep this morning, he'd put on a brown T-Shirt and jeans. That would have to do for their impromptu visit. He fluffed his hair a little and stepped up to the door as they knocked again.

He twisted the knob and opened it. "Good morning. A bit early for a Policeman's Ball funding drive, isn't it?"

The man on the right wore a black fedora hat and appeared to be very cool, but Elmore could tell something brewed under his collar. The man on the left looked nervous, like just being there bothered him.

What is this all about?

"Elmore Ackerman?" the one with the hat asked.

Elmore nodded, not sure if he should be identifying himself.

"Have you seen this girl?" the man with the hat asked. He produced a picture of Sarah Roberts. "She was last seen with this man, Drake Bellamy." He produced another picture of the guy in the cage beside Sarah's.

"Badges please," Elmore said. "I'd like to know who I'm talking to first."

The two men looked at each other. Elmore knew it was the law. They had to identify themselves with their name and badge number. After a brief pause when Elmore thought they weren't going to comply with his request, the man on the left pulled his out.

"Spencer Milton. I'm the lead investigator of the Rogers Centre shooting yesterday, and this here is Rod Howley. He's with the American authorities."

"Pleased to meet you both. To answer your question, I have not seen these two people. I have no idea how this has anything to do with me."

Rod turned around and appeared to scan the property.

"Is there something you're looking for?" Elmore asked.

Rod came back around and stared at him. "As a matter of fact, I am. These two people. And I think you know something about them."

Spencer grabbed Rod's arm. "Rod, that's not how we do it here. There are procedures. We have to follow them."

"Procedures?" Elmore asked. "What are we talking about here? You're looking for two missing persons, and you knock on my door and discuss procedures. What's going on?"

Rod pointed and waved at one of the black and whites. The back door opened, and the security guard from last night who had helped Elmore walk his two prisoners to his car stepped out.

Shit. It's over.

He debated whether or not to slam the front door, walk to his office, grab his two pistols, and shoot every single cop in the face.

The guard stepped closer and tilted his head. The sun was still rising, but it came from behind the house, shining on the guard and casting Elmore in a shadow.

The guard lingered a little longer, then shook his head.

"No, I don't think so. It was dark last night, but I don't think so," he said.

Elmore almost breathed a sigh of relief but stopped himself, knowing they'd hear it.

"Look again," Rod said.

"I did look. The guy last night had a mustache. This guy doesn't."

Rod glared at Elmore and then stepped up to him, staring

at his lips. Spencer grabbed Rod's arm again, but Rod brushed it off.

"Stubble," Rod said. "You have stubble. I wondered if you shaved your mustache off, but you have stubble. It's been at least two days since you've shaved." Rod stepped back and crossed his arms. Elmore could see he was getting quite angry about something.

What brought him here? How could he be so sure?

"Was it someone else, like a brother?" Rod asked Elmore, not letting his gaze waver. "Or did you wear a fake mustache? Wait, don't tell me. It was fake, right?" Rod lifted his knee, slapped it, and laughed as if he'd cracked a fabulous joke.

"Okay, I think this is enough," Spencer said. "We're sorry to trouble you, Mr. Ackerman."

"No trouble at all, but I'm still confused about what this is all about. What brought you to my door?"

Rod's face lost all sense of humor. His eyes bore through Elmore, his lips pursed. "Sarah Roberts brought us here. We're looking for her, and I think you know something about that."

"Rod," Spencer said. "Come on, let's go. We're done here."

"Not yet," Rod said. "Mr. Ackerman. May we continue this conversation inside?"

"It's six in the morning," Elmore said. "You can't be serious."

"I'm. Very. Serious."

"It's not a good time. I won't be bullied by American cops."

Spencer stepped off the stairs and started toward the

black and whites. He stopped and turned back. "You coming, Rod?"

"I know you know more than you're letting on." Rod moved closer to Elmore and whispered, "I'll be back, and when I am, it'll be on my terms."

Rod stepped off the front steps and walked backward, studying the front of the house. He pointed at the roof. "What's that up there?"

He doesn't miss a thing.

"It's a rooftop patio," Elmore said. "I had it built in early 1986 when Haley's Comet made a pass that March. I've always been interested in astronomy. That patio and railing are equipped with a chair that leans back to where I'm almost lying down, and there's a typical alt-azimuth mount for my ten-inch Schmidt-Cassegrain telescope. I even have a Mak-Newt in that baby—from Ceravolo Optical Systems out of Ottawa."

He figured memorizing that astronomy shit years ago would come in handy one day. If he only knew what that tripod mount was really for, he'd arrest me on the spot.

"What does all that mean?"

Is he testing me? Does he know about this stuff?

"What are you doing?" Spencer stepped back up beside Rod. "What has this got to do with anything?"

"Let him answer if he wants to. We're just talking here. No harm."

"It means," Elmore began, "that the secondary mirror is flat and imparts no power as do others."

"You go to all that trouble to build an observatory on your roof — why not have a larger telescope than a ten-inch? Couldn't you just aim that thing out your living room window?"

He's trying to trip me up. Fuck this. I'll bury him one day. Nobody tests me. Ever.

"With telescopes, two contradictory rules apply: the bigger the telescope, the better. The smaller the telescope, the more often you'll use it. Sure, a ten-inch will outperform an eight-inch and so on, but unless I built a huge observatory, a ten-inch is all I need. Contrary to your earlier comment—that's not an observatory. It's a patio, a deck, a veranda—or whatever you want to call it. I use a telescope up there. That's it."

Rod stepped backward a few more steps to get a better look. Then his face lit up like he remembered something. He grabbed his cell phone and dialed.

"Who are you calling?" Spencer asked.

They were far enough away from Elmore's front door that he had to struggle to listen.

Rod held up a finger for Spencer to wait. Then he closed his cell phone and looked between Elmore and Spencer.

"No signal out here."

"That's odd," Spencer said. "We called in just as we hit the driveway."

"I know," Rod said and then whispered something private to Spencer. He turned back to Elmore. "I will return. See you again soon."

Could the American have figured out that I have a cell phone jammer? How?

Something was going on behind the scenes. Something Elmore couldn't put his finger on. But he knew, whatever it was, he had to figure it out, or it would finish him. This American cop was smart.

All the men got into their two vehicles and drove down his driveway, disappearing behind the line of trees at the end of his property.

Elmore slammed his front door and started pulling on his scab. Time was running out. They could get a search warrant and legally walk through his house. He had to do something fast. Everything was over if he fell on the police radar.

But what brought them here?

He ran into his office and grabbed one of the toenails from his container. After slipping it in between his front teeth to flick back and forth, he picked up his TagFinder and slipped it into his back pocket. It was a similar model to the ones used on bar codes at any Wal-Mart, but this one was better. It would locate radio frequencies and signals that many others couldn't. Somehow the cops were on his doorstep this morning because something led them there. Something like a tracking device. It was the only plausible answer. Nothing else made sense, especially after what Rod had said when Elmore asked why they came to his door. Sarah Roberts brought us here. How could she? There was only one way, and because of his signal jammer, whatever led them to his house wasn't working properly. The only proof they had was that no signal worked near the home.

What did that asshole whisper to the other guy?

He opened the bottom drawer of his desk, grabbed the pistol, stuck it in the back of his jeans again, and left his office, Jackie's nail digging into his gums. In the kitchen, he mixed mayonnaise with a can of tuna and pulled out his baggy of dried Special K, or as it was better known, ketamine. After mixing enough to knock Sarah out for a few hours, he spread it on brown bread, cut it in half, added corn chips, and started for the basement.

It was almost seven in the morning. It would take at least thirty minutes to knock her unconscious when ketamine was distributed through food, but he had the time. Rod wouldn't be back until tonight or tomorrow morning. A man like that was too determined. He'd be back, with or without a warrant.

Before opening the basement door, he set the food on the hallway cabinet and looked out the living room window. The front drive was empty.

He turned back to the food and the cabinet it sat on. The third drawer down held an empty syringe. He stuck the tip in and took care to fill it with liquid ketamine. If either of his prisoners caused trouble, he would forgo the food and simply inject them. It would work faster, knocking out a full-grown adult in less than five minutes.

He set the syringe on the tray, picked it up, and opened the basement door.

"Okay, Sarah, time to eat. Then I can have my way with you. We'll find out how these men got here today. I'm sure the answer is inside you somewhere, and I'm coming to find it."

Chapter 23

Sarah sat up when she heard the basement door open. Elmore came down the stairs, a tray in his hands.

"Who was at the door?" she asked. "Morning guests coming for tea or Rod Howley?"

Elmore's eyes twitched in response to what she asked. "Rod and Spencer didn't want to stay too long. They were asking about you, though, which I don't quite understand, but I will in time. Everything in time."

Rod and Spencer? That's great but impossible. No one has those kinds of tracking skills.

But now that Spencer was working with Rod, and they were already at Elmore's door, that instilled a surge of hope. With Rod on Elmore's tail, things could change fast. For a brief moment, she was happy Rod was as tenacious as a shark out for blood.

But how did he do it? Was he psychic like Dolan or Esmerelda? Maybe that's why he's the head of the Sophia Project because he's got a sixth sense. That put a lot of things together for her. How he knew she was in that coffee shop and how he just showed up at the CN Tower.

She thought about Parkman. He had to be going crazy wondering where she was. Why wouldn't he be working with Spencer too? Parkman and his fucking toothpicks. Sarah smiled at the thought.

"What's so funny?" Elmore asked.

She stepped up to the bars and gripped one on either side of her face. "You can't beat guys like Rod Howley. He's too good. That man chased me all over Europe and back here, right to your house. There's no way you're smarter than he is."

Elmore's face twitched, and he looked away. He picked up something from the tray and slid it into his wide front pocket before she could catch a glimpse of it. When he looked back at her, his lips had tightened. Without averting his eyes, he picked up the food tray and bent in front of her cell door. He placed one sandwich on the floor and slid the paper plate under the bars.

He walked over to Drake's cell and did the same.

"You are looking better this morning, Drake. How's the breathing going?"

Drake took in a large breath, smiled, and on the exhale, said, "Fuck you."

"How sweet. Good morning to you, too."

"Drake," Sarah said. "Don't eat anything he gives you."

Elmore stood and walked back toward Sarah's cell door. "So it's like that, is it?" he asked.

He produced a key of some sort and pressed down on it. Sarah's cell door unlocked. She couldn't believe it. All she had to do was get past him, and she could leave.

This'll be so easy.

She braced herself to lunge.

From behind his back, he pulled out a gun.

Shit. That'll confuse things a little.

He aimed it a little left of her head. She saw movement at the trigger.

He's going to shoot that thing!

The gun fired, and a bullet zinged by her head, barely a foot away.

Drake screamed, but she could hardly hear it. Sarah dropped to her butt at the thought that he was about to fire his weapon again. She lost her balance and rolled onto her back, bumping the back of her head on the concrete floor. All she could think to do was drop and roll. Be evasive.

She turned around to see what Elmore had fired at. A small hole in the back wall showed where the bullet had entered. Small pieces of concrete had trickled down to the floor where the hole had formed.

She brushed her hair aside and looked up at Elmore. Would he shoot again? Did he try to hit her?

He knelt close to her. She tried to back away, but her head hurt from kissing the concrete. She couldn't get away fast enough. He jammed his hand into her thigh. She saw the tip of a needle near his thumb.

What the fuck is that?

She screamed and tried to scramble away from him. She hit the back wall, used it to get to her feet, and then pushed off the wall to jump on Elmore. He repelled her easily and stepped back to the cell door with a foolish grin. Then her cell door shut and clicked to lock.

Why am I so weak suddenly? What the hell was in that

needle?

She looked at Drake, but her vision blurred. She felt wobbly on her feet now.

"What have you … done to me?"

Drake banged the bars on his cell. "What have you done? I'm going to kill you. You hear me. I'm going to fucking murder your fucking face."

Sarah slipped down onto the mattress. She felt vertigo and her eyes rolled back in her head.

Then she lost consciousness.

Chapter 24

WHEN DRAKE CALLED SARAH'S name, it pleased her. She smiled, turned onto her side, and woke with a sudden pain in her neck. She opened her eyes and lifted her head up. Blood stained the mattress in the area where her head had been.

What the fuck did that asshole do?

"Sarah," Drake called. "You doing okay?"

She could tell he cared for her from the emotion in his voice. He had feelings for her, and she didn't mind it at all.

Yeah, but nothing goes down between us if we're killed. Gotta get outta here first and in one piece.

She examined the back of her neck for the source of the blood. The stitches where Rod's man had hit her with his baton when she got off the plane in Chicago had reopened.

"Shit, that hurts."

She sat up on the mattress and looked at Drake.

"That guy did stuff to you," Drake said. He appeared to be on the verge of tears.

Now she was fully awake. "What kind of stuff?" she

asked, not sure she wanted to hear the answer.

"He used a knife and cut into the back of your neck."

"Oh, that's it? Nothing else?"

"What do you mean, nothing else? He fucking operated on you, and I couldn't do anything about it."

"But he didn't … you know, touch me?"

"No, nothing like that. He operated on you and then went upstairs mumbling to himself, pissed off about something."

The lock clicked on the door above. It slid open, and Elmore's footsteps came down. Sarah ran her hands all over her body, checking for anything indicating Elmore did more than just cut into her neck. Everything felt fine, except she needed to pee badly.

He could've waited another minute.

"Sarah, you're up," Elmore said. "Glad to see it. We need to talk. Things have changed."

She got off the mattress and stepped to the cage's door. "Tell me what you drugged me with. Then we talk."

"Ketamine. I call it Special K. It's a human tranquilizer. Perfectly safe. Now, I have a question. Are you willingly working with Rod Howley?"

Sarah looked at Drake and then back at Elmore, confused by the question. "No. He wants me to work with him, but the more I refuse, the more difficult he makes my life."

"Are you saying you're not in collusion with him to take me down?"

"Take you down? You're deluded. I've never heard of you before. I came to Toronto for Drake." She stopped and looked at Drake. His eyes widened, and his mouth moved up a little. She was happy to see his eyes had cleared. She turned back to Elmore. "What I mean is, I heard Drake was in trouble. That's why I'm here. Rod tried to keep me in the States."

Elmore moved his armchair within three feet of her cell door and sat down. "So I've been thinking. How did Rod find you so fast?"

"I'd love to know that, too. The bastard feels attached to my hip."

Keep him talking. Listen. Evaluate him. There has to be a way out of here, and I will find it.

"I know you don't have a hidden cell phone that you could've called the police on because of this." Elmore held up a small black device. "This is what they call a Spy Wireless, Wi-Fi Bluetooth Signal Jammer. You can buy one of these babies for just over a hundred American." He turned it in his hands, examining it like he would appraise a diamond ring. "Its frequency range blocks anything for up to thirty meters, which to you Americans is about a hundred feet," he said this last part sarcastically and laughed at his own joke. "It's great for my business because it's portable. I can take it with me to the photo studio. If anyone sends a girl in to record a conversation of mine or open a line on a cell phone to an outside listener, they'll get nothing. I'm free to talk at my place of business without being recorded. This means even if you brought a cell phone with you to your little cage, you wouldn't have been able to call out, as I've had this plugged in down here since you first arrived. I forgot to grab it in my haste to get downtown yesterday." He shrugged and raised his eyebrows. "I fucked up and totally forgot it. That's why I had to toss Drake's cell out of the car."

He set the jammer down, steepled his fingers, and looked back at her. "So I figured they picked up a signal of some kind all the way to my door. That means they had bugged you or had a tracking device on you. When you were unconscious, I asked Drake, and he told me about the tracking bracelet you managed to remove at the Rogers Centre. It didn't make sense at first." He stopped and looked at the concrete ceiling as if he was thinking.

You are the weirdest man I've ever met.

"In case I'm ever electronically bugged," he continued, "my phones, my office, whatever, I have this little baby." He held up a different device. "It's a TagFinder. This device searches for and locates things that are emitting a radio signal. And voila. Wouldn't you know it? In the back of your neck, I found a VeriChip."

Sarah reached up to feel where the stitches were. She put it all together instantly.

So that's what Rod did. He pulled my hair to cause pain and had his henchman hit me so I wouldn't ask why the stitches were in my neck.

"What's a VeriChip?" Sarah asked.

"The VeriChip is a human transplantable tracking device. Although yours was modified for GPS tracking. Quite genius, really. That led me to believe you were working with Rod. How the hell could he have gotten that thing in your neck without you knowing about it? I mean, come on, you're Sarah Roberts. You are fast becoming a legend in the media."

She remembered waking in the interrogation room, feeling that maddening headache, and having to chew Advil. Then she felt the stitches.

That bastard.

Now she knew what their plan had been from the beginning. And the tracking bracelet for her wrist was like some childish decoy.

She looked at Drake. The understanding of how Rod had tracked them so well was on his face. She nodded with her eyes ever so slightly that only Drake could notice it.

"The look on your face tells me you're surprised by what I'm explaining to you. Well, let me tell you, I know people. I have a keen sense of what people desire and how emotions play across their faces. Don't worry. The VeriChip has been destroyed. Now Rod will never be able to track you again."

Her stomach dropped. For the first time since she met Rod in that hotel lobby in Budapest, she wanted him to track her now. More than ever.

"How did you destroy it?" she asked.

"The VeriChip is just a little bigger than a grain of rice. They're quite the modern invention, really. I looked it up while you slept. The one in your neck is an RFID transponder encased in a silicate glass."

Sarah held up her hand. "What's RFID stand for?"

"I'm getting to that. Don't interrupt. We have to discuss this, and then I will tell you how I will kill Rod Howley."

Sarah nodded, not liking any of what she heard.

"The PositiveID Corporation, previously known as the VeriChip Corporation, got preliminary approval from the FDA to market its device. It was later revealed the implants could cause cancer. So be happy I've removed yours. It wasn't in long. You still had stitches." He adjusted himself in the chair and leaned back. "The PositiveID Corp stopped marketing their implantable human microchip by mid-2010. But it's still used today. For instance, the VeriChip implant is offered for identifying VIP guests at the Baja Beach Club, a nightclub in Rotterdam, Netherlands, among other places.

Theoretically, you can physically locate a person by latitude, longitude, altitude, speed, and direction of movement with one of these modified babies. The mindset is you could track your kids going to school. Courts could order them implanted into sex offenders to track their whereabouts." He laughed at what he thought was a joke. "And what about missing persons?" He laughed again. "Funny how we're discussing sex offenders and missing persons."

"You didn't answer my question. What does RFID stand for?"

It seemed like Elmore had just stepped into another headspace. He looked at the floor, scratched at something on his head, and zoned right out.

Sarah saw that Drake was wondering what had happened, too.

"That little fucking chip brought the cops to my door," he mumbled to himself, still staring at the floor. "Now I'm on their scope. After all these years … never making a mistake … and now … I have to kill to stay free."

Kill? Rod or us?

He blinked and looked up at her. He glanced at Drake and then back to her. "What did you just say?"

"I asked what RFID stands for."

"Radio frequency identification. You can thank me later when things calm down."

"Thank you for what?" Sarah asked.

"These chips can be dangerous. They pose a continual risk to the subject who is implanted. If you get too close to a large magnet, it could cause adverse tissue reactions. A person could be burned when the chip reacts to an outside source of EMF radiation, such as a strong electrical field. It would cause serious burns inside and out of the subject wearing it."

"How did you destroy it?"

"I used a simple microwave oven. That's all you need. I left it in until it burst into a tiny flame."

A part of Sarah was furious with Rod for implanting her, but another part of her was happy. Rod had his reasons, as devious as they were, but because of the implant, he was about to determine that the last time it emitted a signal was in or near Elmore's house. That meant Rod would be back. Whether the Canadians allowed him to or not, he would find a way. He also knew that showing up at Elmore's door that morning meant she would be gone soon, whether Sarah was there willingly or unwillingly. Rod would have to act fast, and fast for Rod was right away.

At that moment, she'd rather deal with Rod than with the insane man sitting three feet from her cell door.

Elmore pointed at her. "I know what you're thinking. I've thought of it, too. I met Rod, and I know what kind of man he is. I learned a lot watching him handle the other cops and the questions he had for me. I know he recognized the mount I have on my roof, and he knows it's not for a telescope. Rod won't stop. But I'll be waiting. I'll be ready. If he tries an illegal raid, all his men will die, including him. I have it all set up. Everything's covered."

Elmore stood and pushed the chair back against the far wall. He turned around to face her. "Don't worry, Sarah. Rod will be out of your life forever soon enough."

Chapter 25

As Elmore left, he turned out the light, casting the basement into an unforgiving darkness. Drake had heard Sarah use her toilet, but other than that, he couldn't tell if she had fallen asleep or not.

"I'm sorry, Sarah. I wish I could do something. I'm going crazy stuck in here like a prisoner."

"It's not your fault. Rod's coming. He'll take care of Elmore, and then I'll be Rod's prisoner again, but at least his terms are easier to deal with. Besides, if anyone's at fault, it's me. Vivian sent me a warning about a fake cop. I missed it. I assumed it was Spencer. I'm the one who should be sorry for getting you into this."

"Tell me about your sister."

Drake stretched out on his mattress and listened to Sarah's voice's rhythmic tone and beauty. He would pursue her aggressively if they ever got out of this alive. He could easily see them spending many years together.

Sarah told him about her sister and how Sarah herself

hadn't even known she'd had a sister until five years ago. Vivian had been murdered. The murderer was recently killed in a church an hour's drive from Budapest.

Vivian gave Sarah messages, and Sarah acted on them. The messages helped people survive accidents and prevented crimes, but sometimes things went wrong, as evidenced by where they were.

That was the reason Rod wanted her. To perform for him so he could include her in some organization called the Sophia Project.

"But I don't believe him," Sarah said. "I'm sure it has something to do with the war machine. Get enough real psychics on your side, and you could win any war."

"Yeah, sounds like it."

"But, I warn you, be ready. Rod is coming, and things may get a little dicey around here when he does. I'm going to do my best to escape him, too."

"I'll be ready."

After a minute of silence, Drake said, "I don't know why Elmore is keeping me alive. We both know he wants you."

"Probably until the heat goes down. Having an extra hostage can't harm him in the long run."

"Then let's sleep in rotating shifts. He's unpredictable."

"Agreed," Sarah said. "You sleep first. I'll stay awake."

"No. You sleep. You need your rest."

"Is that the way it's going to be with you?"

"What way?"

"Traditional. The man takes care of the woman's shit, like letting me sleep first."

Drake thought about it for a second, not wanting his answer to upset her, but he realized only the truth would work with Sarah. "Yes. It's the only way. A man must respect a woman. She's the one with the tough life. She has to bear children. She has to deal with cramps and other shit on a monthly basis. Women get abused by men who want only one thing. Women get paid less at a job while holding the same title as a man. In my opinion, women have the raw deal. But when I deal with the woman in my life, I will put her on a pedestal and treat her as she should be treated. This is who I am, and that's how I feel about it."

He didn't get a response.

"You asleep?" he asked.

"No, I'm not," Sarah said. "What you said is good. Don't ever change. Good night. I'm sleeping."

Drake smiled to himself. That was easy.

"Oh, and Drake?"

"Yeah?"

"I'm going to give you something to think about. I read once that the reality of psychopaths, homicidal or otherwise, is that they are devious, cunning, and more ingenious and resourceful than the authorities that guard them. Be careful. Be very careful. We are being hunted even in these cages. And remember, fear stands for false evidence appearing real. Just be strong and fight. We'll walk away from this as long as you believe we will. Life doesn't owe you, but it does provide opportunities. You can either watch things happen, make things happen or wonder what the fuck happened. Choose well, and we'll make it. Being defeated is often a temporary condition. Giving up is what makes it permanent. Never give up. I take an interest in my future because I will spend the rest of my life there. You should, too. Now, good night, Drake."

"Good night, Sarah," he said, half dazed by her speech.

Chapter 26

Elmore had stayed awake all night, waiting for Rod to show. He had been positive Rod would try to see inside his house, spy on him somehow, or even attempt to gain access. Without the proper evidence, it would be difficult, but not impossible, for Rod, an American, to get a Canadian search warrant for Elmore's home.

The motion detectors were activated, and Elmore had an earpiece in his left ear, connected to a police scanner, monitoring their traffic in the area. He'd kept the lights in the house off all night and used infrared from his rooftop patio. He'd gone through a pot of coffee and three chocolate bars, but nothing happened as far as he could tell. No one had approached the house. If they had gotten close, they were good. Real good.

They'd have to be Green Berets wearing body-length Kevlar to get past what I've got set up.

In his line of business, not the selling of used panties, but having one or two teenage girls locked in his basement at any given time, he couldn't be too careful.

He patted the underside of both his arms and felt his 9mm Mambas right where they should be, snug in their holsters. Both semi-automatics were loaded with a 15-round magazine. He loved his Mambas, named after an African snake known for its deadly venom that left little to no chance of survival.

When he heard about the Mamba, it was the gun for him. Why else would anyone want a gun unless it's to shoot someone? If you are shooting someone, you want them to have little to no chance of survival.

Elmore scanned the patio where he sat and laughed at how Rod had called it an observatory. It wasn't an observatory in the classic sense. Sure he observed from up there, but not the stars and planets. He observed the grounds surrounding his home. The mount wasn't an alt-azimuth mount for a telescope. It was an M122 tripod for his M60 machine gun loaded with armor-piercing rounds that could defeat Kevlar vests. From the ground, only a serious professional could see the minor differences in the mount.

"If it's good enough for the U.S. military, then it's good enough for me," he whispered to himself in the dark.

He pulled off the infrared glasses and set them down beside him. He yanked the earpiece out and took one more look around his property in the little light as the morning sun began its ascent.

Nothing. No movement anywhere.

"Maybe another day, Rod."

It was time to get some sleep. Later that day, he would deal with Sarah. She needed to start wearing the panties. When he woke up, he would take the first pictures of her wearing the panties, whether she liked it or not. If she didn't work with him willingly, he would shoot her up with ketamine again, but this time he'd use his tranquilizer gun so there would be no need to enter her cell.

He crawled over to the access door, dropped down to the attic, and closed the hatch. Once he got to the main level of the house, he headed for his office, where he placed the Mambas in their holder and put away his infrared glasses. When he stepped into the hallway, something caught his eye. He turned fast but missed it. Something at the rear of the house blinked.

It was more dark than light still, but he was sure he'd seen something.

"Shit, shit, shit!"

He didn't have time for the pistols. He ran back upstairs, climbed the ladder into the attic, and jumped back onto his rooftop patio. He saw them clearly now, without the aid of the glasses, approaching from the rear. The closest one was at least fifty yards out. As the roof was quite high and the patio area had been built in the center, the eavestrough would obstruct his view if they got any closer.

Behind the first man, he counted four more who followed. They were hopping from tree to tree, attempting to stay hidden as they approached.

Elmore looked behind him to ensure no one was coming from the front, but nothing moved there.

He silently lifted the M60 onto the tripod, clicked it into place, and aimed the weapon. He breathed in and out slowly, knowing this approach to intruders could be construed as excessive. But he also knew what these men were doing was illegal. The claim would be that he felt threatened by what looked like paratroopers assaulting his house.

His first priority was to protect the basement at all costs.

He aimed at the man closest and fired. Even from his distance, he could see the man fall. He quickly aimed at the others. Man after man fell in the bush behind his house. The last man remained hidden behind a tree. He waited. Finally, the man stepped out and started running. Elmore took his time to aim due to how far away the man was. He fired his weapon and continued firing until the man was cut down.

He set the M60 aside and surveyed the grounds below him. Nothing moved, and no one returned fire. The sun has eased higher, cresting the trees behind him.

I wonder which one of them was Rod.

He unhooked his weapon from the mount and set it back in its long case.

Below him, somewhere in the house, a glass broke.

"What the fuck?"

Elmore got to the hole and jumped down into the attic. With extreme caution, he crawled down the stairs from the attic onto the second floor of his home. He had to get to his pistols in his office. He had no weapon on him and no way to defend himself.

It has to be Rod.

How did he miss him? He moved along the hall, sweating at the anticipation of a bullet at any moment. Near the end of the hall, he stopped and took long, deep breaths. He had to stay alert and focused. He had to try to not let the fear cause him to make a mistake.

At the corner to the stairs, he slowly peeked around the edge. The stairwell and hall to the kitchen below appeared empty.

This is it. I will be exposed all the way down those stairs, but I have no other choice.

He turned the corner and started down the carpeted steps, one by one, going slow enough to be quiet, fast enough to get to cover.

At the bottom, he breathed out, not even realizing he'd been holding it. With a quick hop across the hallway, he entered his office, where he discovered no one waiting.

He ran over and opened the Mambas' cases. He pulled both out, clicked off their safeties, and held one in each hand. Back at his office door, he felt a lot better. Whoever had entered his house would know the four men out back were dead and that coming here had been met with extreme force. Whoever had entered his home would be frightened, and he intended to shoot them in the face.

Elmore began a systematic search of the main floor and found the point of ingress—the back kitchen door—but he didn't find anyone hiding in any of the available places.

That only left the basement.

He silently walked to the basement door and discovered it unlocked.

A master locksmith, are you, Rod?

He stood to the side and opened the door. He jabbed at the light switch and turned it on. His nerves were playing on him now. It had been at least five minutes since he'd first heard the glass break, and he couldn't stand much more of this tension. Killing those men in his backyard had meant nothing. He'd killed before and actually found pleasure in the act. But the feeling of being hunted in his own house caused him great stress.

He used the back of his forearm to swab at his forehead,

flipped onto his stomach, and edged to the door to look into the basement.

From his vantage point, he could see the bottom front of Drake's and Sarah's cells but not their feet. Something was wrong. They would've heard the door open. Usually, the prisoner stepped forward and awaited Elmore's arrival in the basement unless they were sleeping.

But things were different this time. They had Rod for a visitor.

No one would be joining them. With the cell phone blocker, there would be no way for the visitor in his basement to get the word out for backup. The five-man assault team on his house would have had no legal backing. It was a black operation. Since no one knew the visitor was in his basement and no one would be coming to rescue him, Rod was stuck. Getting past Elmore would be his only option.

He got up, closed the basement door, and locked it. He walked over to the hallway cabinet and maneuvered it in front of the door. The lock was only accessed from the hall side in case a prisoner ever got past him like Jackie had. The remote to unlock it was always in his pocket. Unless Rod, or whoever was in his basement, had a remote, that door would remain locked until Elmore chose to unlock it.

He holstered his two guns and went to the garage, where he grabbed a wheelbarrow. First things first. He would pick up the four dead men in the back and wheel them into his garage for disposal later.

Then he would come back to the basement and deal with the intruder.

Elmore was already working on a plan to flush him out.

He was pretty certain it would work.

163

Chapter 27

THE BASEMENT SETTLED BACK into darkness as Elmore clicked off the light. A flashlight flicked on, and Rod shined it on his face for Drake and Sarah to see him.

"Rod, he's gone for now," Sarah whispered. "But he'll be back. And I've got a question for you."

"Ask away," Rod said.

"Why the fuck did you put one of those tracking devices in my neck? That's over the top, you know. I should be seriously pissed at you—but I'm happy to see you because you're our only chance out of here."

"If I hadn't stuck a VeriChip in you, I think the guy upstairs would be putting something else in you. You're lucky I'm such a bastard."

"He's got a point," Drake added. "He is our chance out of here."

"Where are the keys for these cages?" Rod asked, spanning his flashlight around the basement and stopping on tables and shelves. "And how come my cell phone doesn't work? Do either of you know what the reason is?"

"He always has the keys on him," Sarah said. "It's some kind of electronic device. He uses a cell phone signal-jamming device. It's plugged in over on the far wall."

The flashlight raced along the far wall and found nothing.

"Shit," Rod said. "He must have it upstairs with him."

"What are you going to do?" Sarah asked. "This guy is seriously sick. These cages have a long history."

"What kind of history?"

"A history of females, mostly late teens to early twenties. He's been kidnapping girls and keeping them locked up here for his personal pleasure."

"He's lying. There's no way anyone can carry on that long without any authorities getting suspicious. Impossible."

"Do you really think it's impossible, or are you trying to convince yourself that it is?"

"From what we've seen," Drake added, "we feel it's true. He's ruthless enough to have done it."

Drake gave Rod an overview of what Elmore had told them about his photo studio and how he got the girls here.

"There is something to be said about a man who builds an observation point on his roof and hooks up machine guns to it to cut down anyone who enters his property. He just shot four of my best men. They're outside, either wounded badly or dead. For that alone, I will not let him breathe another day."

Sarah stepped back from the bars of her cell to think. Too bad she had no way to write something. Maybe the recently quiet Vivian would tell her what to do if she could write.

"He'll be back soon," Rod mumbled in the far corner as

he continued searching the basement. "I'll be waiting. Also, he can't know that I don't have backup coming. He will have to assume I do. This'll all be over in no time."

Somehow Sarah didn't believe him.

Chapter 28

ELMORE HAD HANDLED THE four bodies. They were all stacked in his garage, waiting for burial later that day. Elmore removed the belt from one of the men and took another wide walk around the perimeter of his property. Nothing unusual stood out. He'd deal with Rod and then come back up to bury his friends.

He re-entered his house and pulled both Mambas from their holsters.

"Showtime," he whispered to himself.

He shoved the cabinet away from the door and pushed the button on his key fob to unlock it. He moved to the side, in case his visitor stood at the top of the stairs and opened the door, his weapon aimed to fire, the safety off.

But the stairs were empty.

He flicked on the basement light and got down onto his stomach on the cold tile floor of the hallway. He edged around the trim of the basement door and peeked down the stairs. From where he lay, he could see Sarah's ankles and feet and Drake's mid-thigh area. No sign of Rod. Elmore carefully aimed his weapon and fired.

Drake screamed as the bullet hit him in the thigh.

Perfect shot. Yes. Elmore did a fist pump and then shook his head. What is it with that stupid fist pump? Why people did it, he never understood.

He leaned a little farther in and saw Sarah at the edge of her bars, saying something to Drake as he lay on the floor, both hands covering his wounded leg.

He continued to scream as blood seeped out through his jeans.

"The next bullet goes into Sarah," Elmore shouted loud enough to be heard over Drake. "Soon, the two people you came to rescue will be dead. That would make your rescue attempt a moot point, wouldn't it? Then I would have no use for my basement. This door will be shut and not reopened until next month, at which time you'll have expired. Now, the basement is soundproof. There is no escape except through this door, and your bullets won't penetrate it."

He waited a moment to see if Drake would quiet down, then he continued, "But you have a chance to do something good here. You can save Drake by reducing his blood loss. Here's a belt."

Elmore tossed the belt to the bottom of the stairs.

"If you decide to take the belt to Drake, I will open his cell door from here. You are to enter his cell and tie the tourniquet on yourself. Shut the cell door behind you. Do this, and you save all three of you. Don't do this; I will shoot Sarah, lock this door, and leave for a month. It's your choice, Rod. Make it now."

Elmore pulled back a little. He kept one of his guns

aimed down the stairs and his left hand on the doorknob, ready to shove it shut if Rod decided to run for the stairs.

"You're down to seconds left here. It's not a hard decision. Choose now."

"If you unlock Drake's cell," Rod said. "I'll be taking him out and up those stairs to seek medical treatment."

Elmore clicked the button to unlock Drake's cell. He turned and shouted down, "And you'll both be shot before you reach the top. How far can you get with him bleeding like that? Do you think he could still run? You're out of time. Decide."

"Fuck you."

Elmore counted three breaths. Drake still lay on his cell floor, by himself, bleeding out.

He brought his weapon up and aimed it at Sarah. He was out of options. Rod wanted to test him. He learned a lesson. His obsession had been too expensive. Sarah had cost him everything. There were dead men in his garage. An American cop challenged him from the basement. If it meant Sarah had to go, then Sarah had to go. He accepted that his whole operation could not be based on one girl.

He took an extra moment to ensure his aim and fired in Sarah's direction.

She immediately jumped back and yelped.

"Damn, I'm a good shot," he said while picking at the scab on his head.

"Okay, okay," Rod yelled. "Stop shooting."

Elmore could barely hear the word *motherfucker* mumbled, too.

Rod stepped in front of the stairs and glared up at him. Elmore held his weapon steady. Rod picked up the belt and turned around to walk to Drake. Elmore waited until Rod entered Drake's cell, and then he pushed the remote button to lock it.

"Now, discard all your weapons. Toss them away from the cell, or I will come down and execute you all."

Metallic sounds clanged as various pieces of weaponry were tossed through the bars of Drake's cell. He got to his feet, took another deep breath, and started down the stairs. Three guns and two knives lay on the floor by the far wall. Elmore looked at Rod's back as he tightened the belt above the wound on Drake's leg.

He turned to see how Sarah was doing. A small line of blood trickled down her left arm.

"I barely hit you. Damn, thought I'd done worse. Oh well, that works. We're doing panty pics later, so I'll get you a cloth so you can bathe."

"You know," Sarah said. "Your parents should have called you Waldo."

"Why's that?" he asked, wondering if he should smile or not.

"Because when you go missing, it will be hilarious."

"You sure have a big mouth. We'll use that mouth later for a big job. Watch yourself, Sarah. Act accordingly or pay heavy consequences. You and I will either get along, or you'll hate the last year of your life stuck down here waiting for me."

Rod stood at Drake's cell door.

"Pull up your pant legs around the ankles," Elmore ordered.

Rod bent and did as he was told. Nothing there but socks that rose just above the ankle and then flesh.

"Good. I will assume that's all your weapons," Elmore said, pointing at the floor. "If that isn't, I don't have to tell you how bad things will get."

Rod nodded. "That's it."

"All your friends are dead, but you probably already know that. Now, you are all my prisoners. Tomorrow, after I find out whether anyone else is coming or not, I will execute Drake first unless, of course, he does me a favor and dies through the night."

He turned on his heels, grabbed all of Rod's weapons, strode up the stairs, and locked the basement door, the whole time laughing maniacally.

Chapter 29

Rod had done everything to comfort Drake that he could. Drake now lay back on the mattress with Rod's jacket as a pillow. The belt had been loosened and then tied up again to allow circulation to Drake's lower leg, even though the blood loss had slowed some. Rod explained that the leg wound wasn't enough to kill him. But he would need medical attention within a few days to avoid infection and to get the bullet out.

They had talked for hours. It was difficult to know what time it was in the dark. Sarah felt it had to be evening based on how tired she had gotten.

Her wound was so small it wouldn't need stitches. How lucky had she been? As the day turned to what they thought was evening, she told them she'd rest while they stayed awake, and then she would take her turn, staying up through the night while they slept.

Before she nodded off, Rod had apologized profusely at his failure in getting them out. He'd asked if Vivian had been in contact, and Sarah told him the truth. Vivian had been strangely quiet lately, but it might have been on account that Sarah hadn't had anything to write with.

When Sarah woke, she listened but couldn't hear anything from the other cell.

They must've fallen asleep.

That made sense. Why sleep in shifts when they'd all wake fast enough if Elmore came down?

She lay in the dark, trying her best to work on a plan of escape. She couldn't believe what lay before her. How could she have gotten caught so easily again? And what about Drake? She'd finally found a man she could spend time with, and now he'd been shot because of her.

After she saved his life at the ball game, she didn't have to stay on the run with him.

What's that all about?

Why did she? Was he rubbing off on her, or was she rubbing off on him?

She chastised herself. How could she be thinking about Drake at a time like that? She had to figure out how to get them all out of the cages. She could ruminate all she wanted on relationships when she was safe outside Elmore's prison.

The door upstairs opened slowly at that moment. Even though it was dark and her eyes wide, she saw nothing.

The single bulb dangling in front of her cell flicked on.

She closed her eyes, and the plan hit her.

Perfect. It has to work.

She monitored Elmore's movements by the noises he made. He moved with stealth to not wake anyone, making it difficult for her to determine exactly where he was at any given time. For her plan to work, she had to be ready, which meant she had to know where he was.

A subtle scrape of his foot on the floor. A soft crinkle of his shirt. Then nothing.

She lay as still as she could, making sure he would be convinced she was still asleep.

He cleared his throat. He stood close but not inside her cell yet. Her cell door hadn't unlocked.

It'll come at any moment. Just wait. It'll come.

A match scraped across the striker.

Perfect. Here we go.

It landed on her leg and fizzled out. She ignored the pain and didn't flinch or move. She couldn't afford to. This situation was too important. She'd only get one crack at it.

He struck more matches. It sounded like more than one. She braced for the burn.

It almost made her cry out, but she cringed on the inside and counted to five in her head. She made it without showing him any sign that she was awake.

Her heart beat fast, but she forced her breathing to look long and deep.

"Sarah?" Elmore whispered. "Wake up, or I'll keep doing this."

That's what I'm hoping for, idiot.

There was a certain agitation in his voice. Probably not many captives before her defied him like she did. He wouldn't like it. He only wanted compliance.

Well, fuck him.

Another match struck, then a flare-up.

This is it. He's lit a whole book of matches.

He tossed it, and she snapped awake, slid off the mattress, and let the burning book of matches fall to the bed.

Then she grabbed the small fire and brought it down to the edge of the mattress.

"What are you doing?" Elmore screamed.

"Burning your house down. It's over. Everything you own will be gone."

"Noooo," he screamed.

"Too late. We're all going to die here—so I'll burn your house to the ground with a huff and a puff because I'm your big bad wolf."

Sarah blew out softly on the small flames. The mattress was catching, flames licking up the side.

"Stop that! Stop it now, or I will shoot you in the face."

"Go ahead. Better than you touching me." Sarah crossed her arms and smiled. That smug attitude and the I-don't-care-if-I-die façade would drive him crazy.

"Sarah, no. Stop it. We can talk about this."

The side of the mattress, about a foot in height, was aflame and growing. Sarah grabbed the edge of the mattress and lifted it, leaning it against the wall so the rising flames would have the whole length to consume. That's when the lock to her cell door clicked.

Perfect. Here we go.

Elmore headed for the burning bed to stamp out the flames. He didn't get four feet into the cell before Sarah dove at him like tackling a quarterback. She flailed at him, arms pinwheeling, feet kicking.

They rolled, a tangle of limbs. Drake and Rod screamed at her.

She tried for his throat, but he smacked her hand away. With all her weight leaning forward, she attempted to push her elbow down onto his neck.

The burning mattress had become so hot she had to pull her face back. Elmore caught her shift in weight and pushed in that direction, knocking her off. She rolled onto the floor and smacked the concrete wall.

He pulled a syringe out of his side pocket. He lunged at her and shoved the needle toward her thigh, but she pushed off the wall, rolled toward his feet, and missed the tip of the needle by millimeters.

She hit his feet hard, pushed up off the floor, and drove a solid fist into his groin. He yelped out and dropped the needle.

She brought her fist down, braced herself, and punched him again, this time much harder as she had better balance.

Elmore grabbed for his crotch and stared down at her, his eyes wide. He coughed as smoke wafted past his head.

Sarah tried to get to her feet, but he grabbed at her ankles with whatever reserve strength he had. She fell back to the floor beside the mattress, now mostly engulfed.

She tried to crawl away, but he stayed attached. He crawled on top of her legs. She tried to kick at him, but his weight held her legs hostage.

He produced the needle, still intact.

"Oh, no, you don't," she yelled and reached beside her to the burning mattress. She had crawled far enough away from the leading edge of the flames that when she pulled hard, the mattress fell out flat across Elmore's back.

Instantly he let her go of her lower legs as he tried to spin and lift the burning bed off his back. He screamed an inhuman wail as Sarah got up and ran out of the cell, closing the door behind her.

I'm out!

Elmore had managed to slide out from under the mattress, but as it had burned, the small bed had begun to fall apart in chunks. He could no longer push it off as a single unit. He got to his knees and grabbed the burning pieces that still clung to him.

His breath came in ragged gasps, and his eyes watered as he cried. His face shined red where the fire had kissed his skin, with small bits of black in other areas.

Sarah wasted no time. She ran to Drake and Rod's cell and tried their door. It was locked.

Of course.

"Open this door," she shouted at Elmore.

"Never."

His voice grated on her. He wasn't burned badly, but what had happened would leave marks. It was bad enough to need salve.

She stepped back to her cell door. "The keys," she said, her hand extended through the bars.

He reached behind him, nodded slightly, panted, and moved slowly in obvious pain. When his hand came around, it didn't hold the keys.

He had a gun. And now he had a smile on his hideous face.

"Sarah!" Drake yelled.

Sarah reacted. Elmore fired, but she'd already hit the stairs running. He repeatedly fired as she took the stairs two at a time.

Luckily he left the door unlocked at the top of the stairs.

Probably because he came down so quietly earlier, he didn't want to wake us by locking it.

Drake still yelled for her to run. At the top of the stairs, she flicked on all the basement lights.

Elmore was already out of her cell. He pointed his weapon at Drake's cell door.

Rod dove in front of Drake as the gun fired.

Self-preservation stopped Sarah from running down the stairs and ripping Elmore apart with her hands. He had a gun, and she would have a bullet in the face before she reached him.

Elmore pulled on the trigger of an empty gun and started to reload.

At that moment, she thanked Rod under her breath for saving Drake. But now it was her turn to save him. She never thought in a million years she would call the police to help Rod Howley, but that was what she had to do.

As she ran out the front door of Elmore's plush home and hit the front driveway, she shouted, "Vivian, where are you when I need you the most?"

Chapter 30

ELMORE FOUGHT TO STAY on his feet. The pain was more than anything he'd felt before. His mind raced, and his heart beat faster. He had to think. He had to move. Things had gone wrong. It was all crashing down.

Why did I enter her cell?

He couldn't figure out what possessed him to walk into her cell. He had weapons. He could've shot her with the tranquilizer gun. The fire wouldn't have done too much damage to the solid concrete wall.

He just couldn't deal with someone wrecking his property. The fact that Sarah wanted to burn his property had made him angry. He knew, under the influence of rage, he didn't always do the right things, and that's what Sarah had counted on. He knew now that was what she had wanted from the start. To lure him into her cell. He had been wrong with her. He couldn't use strong women as hostages. He only had use for the weak. From that moment on, he committed to himself that he would only kidnap young, weak girls.

If I make it out of this alive and intact.

He stepped closer to Drake's cell and looked in. Rod had taken the bullet to the gut. He lay on the mattress, both hands covering his wound, Drake beside him, adding pressure where he could to his own wound.

Slowly, methodically, Elmore turned for the stairs. Any kind of movement caused pain, so he did his best to go slow.

At the top of the stairs, he cautiously stepped into the hallway in case Sarah waited for him with her own weapon. She was nowhere in sight. In the kitchen, he opened his first aid kit and applied aloe vera gel to as many burns as he could locate on his skin. The cool sensation of the salve calmed the constant burning.

He had to get out of the house. Time was running out. Sarah would be back, and she'd bring help. Based on her statement, they'd have enough information to enter his home with force, and he was in no condition to ward them all off now.

He grabbed his ammunition box, loaded his Mamba, and holstered it. After that, he picked up his computer and the black container of nails in his desk drawer and took them out to his car. Once they were loaded, he headed back into the house for a hostage. The choice had been made for him. He would need one of the two men in the basement to help keep him alive, and he knew which one would be a more powerful hostage.

In the basement, he stepped up to the cell door and looked in at the two men bleeding on his floor.

"You're both staining my floor," he said. "Do you realize how much work it is to get blood out? I should know."

It hit him then. It was truly over. Everything he had built.

All the security measures he had taken. The system of stealing girls out of their comfortable lives and placing them into his. All over. Everything changes, but he didn't think his lifestyle would change this fast. He thought he could go on for years to come. But Sarah Roberts had stopped him by simply escaping.

He would have to move. Not just another city but another province, maybe even another country, and he would have to do it fast. Within twenty-four hours, the police would be hunting him everywhere.

"Fuck!" he shouted.

Sarah will pay dearly for what she had done. At least his company would survive. He had money, and it continually flooded into his account on a weekly basis. Maybe he would move to Japan and get lost there for a while.

If Roman Polanski can do it, so can I.

Elmore pushed the button to open Drake's cell door. He motioned with his Mamba for Drake to stand on his one good leg. Drake did as he was told, hopping, the pain displayed on his face.

The blood coming out between Rod's fingers seemed to increase in speed.

"You're losing a lot of blood, Rod. I estimate you have an hour left, maybe less. How does that make you feel? Do you regret coming to my home?"

Rod shook his head.

"Why's that? Why do you not regret it? You're dying, you fucking pig."

"Because I got to see Sarah again. And now she's free. That's all that concerns me. She's my life's mission."

Elmore felt confused. "You justify your death this way?"

"It's complicated." Rod's voice weakened.

"How so?" The man had to go, but Rod's statement intrigued him.

Rod looked at Drake. "When you get away from him, take good care of Sarah. She needs a man like you."

Elmore lifted his weapon and aimed it at Rod's face. "Don't talk to Drake. Tell me why it's complicated, or you will eat this bullet."

Rod looked down at his stomach and moved his eyes along the stream of blood. He looked back at Elmore and then at Drake. "I love Sarah. Always have, although she had no idea. That was one of the reasons she became my sole mission. I couldn't let her out of my sight." He winced. "Tell her I'm sorry, Drake. I did it to protect her, so nothing like this would happen. She'll understand. Tell her that was why I got so angry at Rosalie in Hungary. I thought she put Sarah in harm's way."

"I'll tell her," Drake said.

Elmore lowered his gun. "Town is far from here. Sarah doesn't have a phone. The police couldn't possibly be here within the hour, and you're going to bleed out by then. I will not make your death quick. Goodbye, Rod. Enjoy the afterlife."

Elmore pushed Drake toward the stairs. They made it to the hallway and then the front door. Elmore stepped out first to scan the area, not worried that Drake would try to run away.

The area was serene, with nothing moving. He guided Drake to the rear of his car and opened the trunk.

"Get in."

Drake rolled into the trunk without protest.

Elmore got behind the wheel and left his property via the back way, vowing to himself to never return again.

187

Chapter 31

IT PAINED HER HEART to leave Drake behind. The chance that Elmore would kill both men and leave was very high. She only hoped that he would take a hostage. Being a hostage and alive was better than not being a hostage and dead.

She got to the end of the driveway and ran along the shoulder of a two-lane highway. Traffic raced by as people drove into Toronto for the day's work.

She waved and leaned into the road at every passing car, attempting to get their attention. After the fifth car had passed, she stepped into the road in front of a small Honda Civic. The sun had gotten high enough for her to be seen without headlights.

The Honda slowed and pulled onto the shoulder beside Sarah.

"Is everything okay?" the female driver asked.

"Do you have a cell phone?" Sarah asked. "I need to use it. I don't want a ride. I just need to make an emergency call. Do you have a phone?"

"Who doesn't nowadays? Come on, get in."

Sarah ran around to the passenger side, jumped in, and shut the door. The driver turned on her four-ways and handed Sarah a small pink phone.

"Are you okay? Did you run out of gas?"

"Not really. You'll hear everything when I make this call."

She had considered staying in the house and attacking Elmore on her own but decided he was too crazy and had too many devices, like the tranquilizer gun and needle. Vivian hadn't offered her any notes on Elmore, so she wondered if her odds would be better with the police going in and dealing with him legally.

She watched the driveway as she dialed the police.

She needed to distance herself from that basement and what had gone on with the other victims. As a woman, it was too much to handle all at once.

The line at emergency services rang.

"Police," she said after being prompted. Then, "I need to speak to Spencer Milton, the lead investigating officer of the Rogers Centre shooting. I have information for him. Tell him my name is Sarah Roberts. Yes, I will wait."

The woman sitting beside her put both hands on the steering wheel. Her right leg started tapping up and down. As she checked her mirrors, Sarah caught the driver's head moving back and forth.

"It's okay," Sarah said to comfort her. "Don't worry. None of this will come back to you. We're the good guys."

The driver nodded, but Sarah could see this was bothering her.

The line clicked, and then she heard, "Spencer here. How

do I know you're Sarah Roberts?"

"Drake told me about you. He filled me in on Monika and how you stopped her at the lake. Listen, I need you to locate a cop friend of mine. He's the only one I trust. He's in Toronto and will be pissed that I wasn't on that plane. I need his help. His name is Parkman."

"Hold on," Spencer said.

There was a pause where it sounded like the phone was being jostled. A large truck passed by, and the little Honda shook. Sarah snuck a glance at the driver. She didn't look any better.

"Sarah?"

Parkman.

"Parkman. Listen, I have a problem."

"Right to business, I see. I was worried, you know."

"You think I did this on purpose?"

"Never. Where are you? I'll come to get you. What's this? Do they want to charge you with murder? And who was Joseph Singer anyway?"

"That's nothing. Rod made it up."

"He doesn't know you very well, then."

"Ask Spencer where I am. He came to the house yesterday."

Parkman pulled the phone away and then back. "He says he knows exactly where you are but doesn't know why you're there."

"Long story—but you have to hurry. Drake is in the basement with a gunshot wound to his leg, and I think Rod got shot badly, too. Elmore may be on the run, but I haven't seen him leave his property yet. Bring everything you got and … just get here."

Hope filled her eyes in the form of tears.

Chapter 32

SARAH HANDED THE PHONE back to the driver. She offered a reassuring smile and stepped from the vehicle. The little Honda sped away, kicking up a few stones off the shoulder.

She found a spot just inside the woods where she could sit and wait while still able to see Elmore's driveway entrance.

In less than ten minutes, she heard the sirens in the distance.

Good, this is finally coming to an end.

She walked back out to the road, and a brown car in the distance came her way. The vehicle had to be going at least a hundred miles an hour. An ambulance trailed it.

Sarah waited until no other cars were visible and walked across the road to meet the unmarked cruiser.

Parkman jumped out, a toothpick sticking out of the corner of his mouth.

Some things never change.

"You okay?" he asked.

"Yeah, but I could've used your help a couple of days ago."

"I didn't know where you were. I'm here now. Jump in and brief us on what to expect when we enter this home. We're going in right now."

Spencer offered her a more welcoming smile than she deserved after stealing Drake from his protection and running away with him. He started the car up Elmore's driveway while Sarah told them more details about Drake and Rod and their wounds. She explained the cages and what Elmore had been doing in the past. She added that he ate fingernails, which got a strange look from Parkman, who then rolled his window down a little and spit his toothpick out.

There was no movement at the front of the house as they got close.

"His car was here when I ran out the front door. I don't know how he got past me. I watched his driveway while I waited for you guys."

Spencer stopped the car, and they all got out, both cops with guns already in their hands. The ambulance stayed back fifty meters, and no paramedics exited.

"Stay out here," Spencer said.

Sarah nodded. Gladly. Too creepy in there.

She wasn't the trained professional in these situations that the two men approaching the house were.

In the distance, it sounded like a whole platoon of cop cars were en route.

Spencer and Parkman stood on either side of the front door for the count of three, and then Parkman stepped out, kicked the door, and disappeared inside. Spencer followed him.

Sarah sat down in the back seat of the cruiser, leaving the door open. She waited a full minute before she couldn't handle it anymore. If Elmore's car was gone, then so was he. That meant no danger, and Drake and Rod needed that ambulance.

She got up, walked to the front door, and entered the main foyer. Spencer saw her from the kitchen.

"I thought I told you to stay outside."

Parkman stepped between them from an office. "You think you can get Sarah to do what you want?"

Spencer started up the stairs, his weapon held high. Parkman opened the basement door.

"Be careful," Sarah said.

Parkman nodded. "Hello? Anyone down there?"

They both listened but heard nothing.

Parkman got down on his knees and brought his head close to the ground to see as far into the basement as he could. He looked at Sarah. "All I see is the front of two prison cells like cages. In the one on the left, it looks like Rod. The one on the right is empty."

"You don't see Drake?"

He shook his head.

Sarah stepped past him and started down the stairs. Parkman grabbed her arm.

"Hey, wait, let me go first."

"The car is gone. Drake is gone. That means Elmore's not here. We're safe."

A cacophony rose from the front of the house. Parkman and Sarah turned to see a line of uniformed police officers entering the front door.

"Backup's here."

Sarah stepped away from Parkman and down the stairs. She reached the open door to Rod's cell and ran to him.

"Where's Drake?"

Rod's eyes opened halfway. His skin was pale, and he looked sleepy.

"I need an ambulance in here," Sarah shouted toward the stairs. "Now!"

She turned back to Rod and lifted his head. "It'll be okay. We'll get you out of here. You did well. You saved Drake's life. We'll find him, we'll find him."

Parkman came up behind her. "Paramedics are coming in now."

She nodded at him. Then she leaned in closer and asked Rod if there was anything he could tell them that would help. She caught the slight nod of his head. She leaned in closer to his mouth to listen.

"They left … ten minutes ago. He has … Drake."

Sarah turned and looked at Rod. "Okay, I'll get him. You take it easy. Here come the doctors. Go get healthy now, okay? We'll see you when you're better."

Two paramedics rushed in. Sarah held his head a little longer and then got out of the way.

Parkman started for the stairs, and Sarah followed, leaving Elmore's basement behind. Just before she reached the top of the stairs, she looked back at the cell she had been in and saw the brown box of panties in the back corner that Elmore had given her to wear when she arrived.

Disgusting.

The police would dig up everything they could on Elmore. That meant digging up the property surrounding his home and letting his victims have proper burials. Maybe then they could rest in peace.

In the kitchen, Spencer was on his cell phone asking someone on the other end for everything they had on an Elmore Justin Ackerman. He said he needed it yesterday and then dropped his phone into his suit jacket's inner pocket.

Parkman and Spencer debated where Elmore would've taken Drake. Sarah listened as they covered public transportation like trains leaving Toronto, the Greyhound Bus, or even the Toronto International Airport.

We're running out of time. Drake's life hangs in the balance.

Sarah hadn't eaten since she had gotten to Elmore's. Her stomach growled, and she bent a little at the pain. She had to eat soon but wouldn't eat anything from Elmore's kitchen.

"This is such shitty luck," Spencer said as he slapped the countertop beside him. "Drake just got away from Monika and her sick family with his life, only to be kidnapped by a psycho. Now he's a hostage somewhere, and we can't even catch a break." He stopped talking when his face lit up with something. "Maybe this has something to do with Ferenci? He may still be involved."

Sarah looked down at her shoes. She'd completely forgotten about the guy who wanted to kill Drake at the baseball game.

"Sarah?" Parkman said.

She looked up at him.

"Can Vivian help us with this?"

She shook her head. "I haven't heard from Vivian in days. She's been strangely silent."

"Why's that?"

"I don't know, but I'm sure she'll tell me soon enough.

What I do know is"—she held a finger up—"where Elmore took Drake. I think I've figured it out. Parkman, Spencer, bring a couple of men, and let's go. I'll tell you everything on the way."

Chapter 33

Spencer drove south toward Toronto, the car's lights flashing on the roof. He took liberties with his driving that only cops could, driving on the wrong side of the road at times and running red lights.

Sarah observed from the back seat, a place she hated to be under any other circumstance. The rear seat of a cop car always sucked.

"Are you sure Elmore didn't say anything about the location of his studio?" Spencer asked.

Sarah shook her head. "No, I'd remember. He said nothing about where it was, only what he did there to the girls."

"I called it in," Spencer said. "I've got my best guys working on Elmore's public records to find what properties or businesses he may own and where they are."

"All I remember is that it's downtown Toronto."

"We're hitting the top of the 427 South, so we'll be downtown in five to eight minutes. Hopefully, my guys will get me something by then."

Parkman sat beside her. He leaned closer. "You doing okay?"

She nodded. "Yeah."

"You know, after what happened in Europe, I was pretty scared when you didn't come off that plane. I called everybody I knew and called in any favors I could but came up empty. I heard nothing about you being in Toronto until you showed up at the Rogers Centre. How could Rod be that powerful?"

"That's the crazy thing about people like Rod. Too much power and no accountability, no consequences. Rod has no governors, nothing holding him back."

Parkman nodded and looked out the window. After a moment, he glanced back at her. "Why do you think Vivian has been silent? In Europe, she was getting even more involved. She made you pass out just to keep you from being shot."

"I know. It's confusing, but I have a theory."

"What's that?"

Sarah looked down at her hands. "Her original goal has always been to catch Armond Stuart. She gave me a couple of safe tasks to accomplish before going after Armond. Once I'd boosted my confidence, I was ready, and she knew it. Now that Armond's dead, she's done. She can rest in peace."

"Okay," Parkman interrupted. "What's next?"

"That's just it. There's been a lot of danger along the way. Many times she'd lead me to the fight, but it was me who did the fighting. I just feel that her job is over now that Armond is gone." Sarah met his eyes. "I might not hear from her again."

"You really think so?"

She nodded.

"Then why send you after Drake? How does he fit in?"

"Because he would've been another casualty of the fraudulent immigration ring that Armond was a part of. If she could save one more life …"

"I disagree," Parkman said. "She did send you to save Drake, but it also netted you Elmore, who, from what we're gathering, is quite the disgusting psychopath. He's preyed on women for too long. If you didn't come to Toronto, Elmore would still be doing what he's been doing for years."

Sarah thought about it for a second. "Maybe you're right. And maybe I came not just to save Drake but to be with Drake."

"Be with Drake? What does that mean?"

Sarah looked away. What she felt inside was so foreign to her that she didn't know what her face would show Parkman.

The radio in the front seat crackled. Spencer clicked a button and talked rapidly.

"Got it!" he shouted.

"Got what?" Sarah asked.

"We know Elmore's studio is in the Entertainment District at the corner of Duncan and Richmond Street. Units are on their way, but they've been ordered to stay back a few blocks until I give the go-ahead. We'll be in that area in minutes. Hold on."

<h1 style="text-align:center">Chapter 34</h1>

ELMORE SLAPPED THE STEERING wheel hard. "Why did I think I could ever control someone like Sarah? Fuck, she has single-handedly ruined everything I'd spent years building."

It further infuriated him that he couldn't find a parking spot. Downtown Toronto on any given day was always a test of patience, and today, Elmore had little. After circling for an hour, he found a parking lot that allowed him to park near the back by workmen tearing up a street.

Summertime in Toronto wouldn't be summer without construction going on all over the place.

Then he smiled to himself. Drake lay in the trunk. The jackhammers were cutting into concrete fifteen feet from his car door. No one would be able to hear Drake with the cacophony of men at work. Elmore had stopped on the way downtown and pulled into the back of a gas station to put duct tape over Drake's mouth and cuffs on his wrists. With enough shouting, Drake would attract someone's attention from the trunk soon enough if his lips weren't sealed.

Taking one final look around, Elmore got out, locked his car doors, and started walking the two blocks to his studio. He'd always kept the studio legal and aboveboard, so it covered his ass with the tax man. There had to be something to explain the income from Japan and how it got generated in the first place. Because it was registered to him, the cops would find it easily, but would they come there first? He felt they'd focus on his house first.

Maybe he needed to call a lawyer. He had the money. He could stop the cops from entering his house. He needed a lawyer to deal with probable cause, search warrants, and illegal entry. They'd have enough to charge him right away if they searched his house. An investigation would ensue, and that's where things would get worse.

Perhaps he shouldn't have left the house. When Sarah ran away and disappeared so quickly, his urge was to get out and get out fast. But if he were still at home, he'd be able to stop illegal searches. Would Sarah's word alone allow them to walk into a private residence? How long did search warrants take to process?

"Damn her," he said out loud.

Two women wearing business suits and carrying briefcases walked by and looked at him.

He passed them and didn't look back. Fuck them if they think he's crazy.

When everything was over, he would hunt Sarah down and find her. Whatever it took, he would catch up with her. But he would only want one thing from her then: to watch the last breath cross her lips.

It's too late now. You've run. You have to keep running. Who knows what's going on back at the house?

The front of his studio looked normal. No one watched him or his premises. He waited a full two minutes and then ran across Duncan Street to the side of the building.

The L'Amore Photo Studio sign sat with pride on the door. For a brief moment, he reminisced about all the beautiful young things which had walked through that door. How many had he taken home and used for pleasure for so many wonderful years? He couldn't remember. Those were the days. Now his studio would serve as a temporary shelter for his captive before he fled to the airport to leave the country. Maybe he should think about going to the Hamilton International Airport, taking a domestic flight to Vancouver, and then flying internationally. Would they monitor every airport across the nation for one man?

After looking up and down the alley and satisfying himself that no one watched, he fished out his keys and inserted them into the door. The lock clicked. Elmore pushed the door open fast and stepped up to the alarm panel to enter the four-digit code to deactivate it.

But the alarm panel remained unlit.

Did I forget to arm it the last time I left?

He'd only forgotten once before. He was very anal about things as serious as that. There was no way he had forgotten. Couldn't be. Someone had to have turned it off, but who?

There was no way the police could already be here and break into his business just to re-lock the door and let him walk in.

So who was here?

He turned around slowly and surveyed the main foyer area. Two doors led to the back. One was the staging area photo room, and the other was a hallway that ended at the bathroom. The little light coming in from the outside was enough to see into each doorway.

"Hello? Anyone here?"

Someone knocked on the door. Elmore jumped and snapped his head toward the door, his heart suddenly beating as fast as the jackhammers by his car.

Fuck!

If it were the cops, they would've seen him enter. If it wasn't cops, then who could it be?

Curiosity drove him to step up to the door and grip the handle. He took a couple of deep breaths and pulled the door open.

A man in a long trench coat filled the door, each shoulder brushing the doorframe.

"Can I help you?"

Elmore thought about grabbing his gun.

Something cold touched the back of his neck. He jerked away and spun to look at who was behind him. An old man, probably in his sixties, aimed a long gun at Elmore's face.

"What the fuck—"

The man in the doorway shoved Elmore farther into his studio. The old man with the gun moved out of the way.

"You are a stupid human being," the old man said.

"Who are you people?" Elmore asked. "What are you doing at my studio?"

"Who I am doesn't matter. I'm here for Drake. Where is he?"

"Who the hell is Drake? This is a photo studio. I have shoots planned for this afternoon."

The old man looked at the large man in the overcoat and nodded. The huge man stepped closer, lifted his arm, and brought his fist down hard and fast. So fast, Elmore didn't have a chance to move. The brick of a fist connected with his nose. A blinding flash of light swept across his vision, and pain erupted throughout his face. He felt the gush of blood before he saw it. Both eyes watered to the point where the men standing before him were blurred. He could not believe the pain. His face was on fire.

"Why did … my nose … broken," he said with a nasal voice.

"We are out of precious time. Where is Drake?"

The guy had a hard accent. Central Europe. Romania or Hungary. What would he want with Drake?

Elmore stepped back and leaned against the wall. His vision hadn't cleared, and his equilibrium wavered. He wasn't sure if he could remain standing. The pain was overwhelming.

"Look, Elmore," the old man shouted. "The police just announced that they were on their way here. Sarah Roberts is coming with them to examine your photo studio because they believe this is where you fled with Drake. I'm thinking we have two, maybe three minutes before they arrive. Tell me where you have left Drake, and I will make it easy for you."

The pit in Elmore's stomach grew. It was truly over. There was nothing he could do now. It could take them a week to locate his car parked blocks away. By then, Drake would be dead. His final act would be to never reveal where Drake remained hidden.

He smiled at the old man and said, "Fuck you," blood spitting out with his words.

The old man leveled his weapon and fired. Elmore fell, unable to hold himself up on one leg. Momentarily, the pain in his face forgotten, he wiped his eyes and looked at his ruined knee. The bullet had entered the top of his right knee. The bottom of his leg sat at an odd angle.

The old man standing over him showed nothing on his face like sorrow, shame, or guilt. He stared at Elmore with anger and the will to continue shooting.

The pain in his leg amplified with each breath. Elmore vomited twice before he got his breathing under control. Blood still ran down the front of his face, and now it seeped through his pant leg.

"Last time. Where's Drake? No more chances."

Elmore stared at the two men, stunned. How did it come to this? Who were these people? What had he gotten himself mixed up in?

He opened his mouth to answer but realized he'd waited too long. The old man had brought his weapon up again and pulled the trigger as Elmore shouted for him to stop.

The bullet punched his other leg. Aghast, Elmore stared at the hole where his other knee had once been. He threw up again, but not much came as his stomach was empty. Vomit mixed with the blood from his nose.

I'm going to die here.

The old man knelt by his head. "My friend here wants to call you an ambulance. You won't die from these wounds if you're taken to a hospital quickly. I've heard they can do wonders with artificial knees nowadays. The other option is you continue to refuse my request, and I will be forced to use the next bullet on your eye hole. So, decision time—bullet in the eye or ambulance?"

Elmore didn't have to think long. "Ambu … lance," he managed to say through the blood entering his mouth.

"Good choice. Then where is Drake?"

"In my car," Elmore said, reaching into his pocket for his keys. His legs shifted with the movement, and he winced and moaned. The brute in the long coat ripped the keys from his hand.

"Where's your car?" The question came out as an order.

"Two blocks from here. By the road construction … jackhammers."

The pain took over. All he felt was pain. His thoughts were scattered. What was happening? What would life be like now?

The old man said something about waiting for Sarah. Park the car on Queen Street. Wait there. They would murder her and Drake as soon as they left the area.

At least Sarah will finally be dead, Elmore thought.

He lay back, his head sliding down the wall and bumping off the baseboard until it landed on the tiled floor. An odd thought struck him about the day he tiled the floor and how the first girl he kidnapped had walked in, a modeling portfolio under her arm. She had glowed in the sunshine. His first sex slave.

Memories, what memories.

Something covered his vision. He forced his eyes open to see what was happening. The old man had brought the gun up in front of his face.

Did he have more questions?

He heard the gun go off, but he couldn't see anything anymore. More pain entered his consciousness. His body convulsed. He tried to shout, but nothing came out.

In the distance, he heard another crack of the gun.

Chapter 35

Spencer raced down Queen Street and parked along the curb. Sarah's stomach growled at the sight of the Korean restaurant on the left and the Indian restaurant on the right.

"We'll leave the car here and walk to the studio. Parkman, we've got dozens of uniforms within one block waiting for me to give the okay to move in." He turned to Sarah. "This is almost over. We'll get Drake out. He's my friend, too."

They all got out and started down the busy street. Pedestrians clogged the sidewalk. The threesome had to separate and walk around people at times. It wasn't until they turned down Duncan Street that they got away from the bustling activity on Queen Street.

Spencer slowed and peeked around at the corner of the building that housed the photo studio. He turned back to Parkman and Sarah.

"No car in the lane."

He stepped out into the open and walked along the alley

to the photo studio's door, where he stood against the wall to the right. Parkman walked over and stood on the left. Sarah stayed back by the entrance to the alley.

Spencer tried the door. It was locked. She was close enough to hear him radio someone who had been set up to watch the front of the building.

"Nothing. No movement your way," she heard through the small speaker.

The two cops walked around to the front and tried two other doors. Everything was locked up tight. No way in.

"It doesn't look like anybody's here," Spencer said. "Maybe they didn't even come this way. Fuck." He slammed his fist into his palm. He turned to Sarah. "Is there somewhere else you feel he could've taken Drake?"

Sarah shook her head. "Nothing."

I could really use your help here, Vivian.

"Maybe we need to get to the airport," Spencer suggested.

His radio crackled.

"Spencer, go ahead."

"Elmore Ackerman's vehicle has been located two blocks from your location."

"Okay, watch the vehicle and call me if anyone approaches it. Otherwise, wait for my call."

Spencer put the radio away.

"He's here," he said to Parkman and Sarah. "I'd bet on it now. We're going in."

Spencer knocked on the studio door. Parkman took up a position beside the door and waited. After no one answered, Spencer knocked again and shouted, "Police, open up!"

No answer. Spencer stepped back, aimed his revolver at

the locked door handle, and fired twice. The knob shattered, and the door popped an inch.

Spencer pointed at Sarah to hang back. He motioned to Parkman to follow him and counted down to three with his fingers. Then he kicked the door and rushed in, his gun ready. Parkman followed.

Two uniformed cops turned the corner behind Sarah.

"They're in there," she said and pointed at the open door.

"We know. He asked us to get you out of the alley."

"Oh, yeah?" Sarah asked. "Well then, we can wait until he comes out and asks me himself."

No way I'm just walking away with *cops* anymore.

"No, you're to be moved to the end of the alley. Let's go."

The cop grabbed her arm and started to lead her away. She snapped her arm out of his grip and stepped back.

"Ever since I've been in Toronto," Sarah said, the anger rising like a tide of boiling water. "Cops have been touching me and telling me what to do. Now I'm getting pissed." She stared at each man and added, "Touch me again. I dare you. Just one more time."

The police had been ordered to stay back. If Spencer had brought her this far, he would've stepped out of the building to make a request of her. These guys were not who they said they were.

The one who'd grabbed her arm pulled out a weapon so fast she didn't have time to call out Spencer or Parkman.

He stepped into her, placed the weapon's tip on the underside of her chin, and said, "A bullet will enter your brain if you call out. Any wrong move, and you'll die. The only thing that'll keep you breathing for the next few minutes is to start walking. Now go."

Chapter 36

THE TWO COPS WALKED Sarah to the end of the alley toward Queen Street. The sweat beading her face wasn't because of the hot sun but her anger. She was sick and tired of people having the attitude that they could do whatever they wanted. No one person owned the world, and no one owned Sarah.

She'd been lucky during the past five years, making it out of scrapes and staying alive with the help of her sister. But Vivian had told her nothing about Elmore or the two men on either side of her. She had no idea what to expect. The men with her were more dangerous than average bad guys because of their carefree attitude. To wear Toronto police uniforms in public and snatch her not ten feet from Spencer and Parkman took balls. These two had no fear. She was sure if she had called out and Spencer or Parkman had stepped from the photo studio, one of the two men in each of her arms would've shot them.

Just before they broke the cover of the alley, the uniform with the gun holstered it. A car idled by the curb, its back door open.

She was out of options. She had to do something. Getting into that car meant death. Better to get shot outside the car, in public, than to enter the car and be executed miles away with no witnesses.

They shoved her toward the door. The man on her left moved away to walk around the back of the car to get in on the other side.

It was her last chance.

She made to enter the back seat and then dropped to one knee in front of the open door. She pivoted fast and swung her other leg into the back of the knee of the guy still with her. His knee shot forward, bumped the car door, and he dropped.

As he fell, Sarah lay down on her back and rolled under the car. She stopped rolling and slid her butt along until she was dead center of the chassis, the exhaust pipe two inches from her nose.

How does this shit always seem to happen?

Who were they? Did they work for Elmore? That couldn't be possible. What Elmore did had to be kept to himself, or he couldn't have gotten away with it that long.

She looked left and right, rolling her head back and forth on the concrete, searching for her aggressors' feet.

The car jerked. Then the driver hit the gas. She turned her head sideways just in time. The edge of the muffler came within millimeters of tearing the top of her nose off.

Both fake cops stepped up and stood over her, guns drawn. No one in the street would question their authority. They were in uniform. They had weapons. Their person of interest had tried to flee. She had assaulted one of them. It would look justified to arrest her with this kind of force. She was all out of ideas.

She raised both hands and said, "Okay, take it easy. I'll go quietly. Thought that might work. Who knew?"

"Shoot her in the face," the uniform on the left whispered.

"Too many witnesses," the other one said, frowning. "Just get her up and in the car."

Vehicles continued to meander by on the street beside her, oblivious that she was being kidnapped in broad daylight on the downtown streets of Toronto with a heavy police presence less than a block away.

The last option she had was a bullet. She'd been shot before. She'd survive. Getting into that car was certain death. She felt it on every level of her soul. Being shot left options.

She got up and was ready to rush them.

A small crowd of pedestrians walking by had stopped to watch the live action.

A man stared at her. He was at least six feet tall, and it was quite evident that he worked out religiously. She pointed at him and shouted, "Help! These men are not cops. They're trying to kidnap me!"

The man shook his head and started to walk away, just as Sarah had wanted. She would've been surprised if he had stepped in to try to help.

The fake uniforms turned to see if he would do anything. Instead of rushing them, she ran five feet to the right and stepped into traffic. A small Nissan swerved to miss her, turning toward oncoming traffic. The car going the other way veered to avoid a collision but swerved toward Sarah.

She couldn't get out of the way in time.

All she could do was jump. Her jump wasn't high enough to clear the hood.

The vehicle had already slowed down. When her foot hit the top lip of the hood, her body rotated sideways as the windshield rushed up to make contact with her back. Several feet later, the car stopped, and Sarah flew off the hood and onto the sidewalk, rolling until she ended up face down.

She breathed in and out in small gasps. Aches and pains came from everywhere, but she didn't move. She did a mental inventory of her body and was pretty sure nothing got broken.

People gathered around her. Someone said not to move her for fear of further damage. Someone shouted for an ambulance.

There was too much attention. No way the uniforms would try to take her now. It would be routine to have an ambulance attend.

She opened her eyes in time to see the uniforms getting into the car they had tried to force her into.

I did it, but I must find a new way to live. Jumping in front of cars just to avoid getting killed is fucked up.

She rolled onto her back and tried to get up to the protests of everyone around her.

"I'm okay, really, I'm okay—"

The people around her were knocked sideways by a shockwave. Someone fell over her legs as she tried to right herself to see what had exploded.

Four car lengths away sat the car the cops had tried to get her into, fully engulfed in flames. No way the driver or the two uniforms had gotten out.

Her stomach clenched at the thought that she was almost

in that car and had also been under it moments ago.

Her stomach wanted to release its meager contents. She rolled to the side and got to her feet, a hand on her abdomen. Most of the people surrounding her had moved toward the burning car. A tattoo shop had lost all its front windows in the explosion.

Holy shit. I'd be dead right now. That was too close.

Who were these people? Who would kill in the open like this? Definitely not people like Elmore. They did it in private, and they preyed on the weak.

A thought raced through her mind like a power surge hit her. She jolted and stared, wide-eyed.

Ferenci and people of Armond Stuart's ilk. The immigration fraudsters. The people after Drake. They're here and after her, too, because she stopped them at the baseball game. Cops on the payroll. She would be a target because she took out their leader in Montone, Italy.

She cautiously stepped backward until she touched the nearest building wall. She felt exposed in the open and with no weapon.

Her left knee ached too much to walk without a slight limp. She'd torn her jeans at the knee. Her elbow was bleeding.

She edged along the building toward the alley's entrance. As attentive to her surroundings as she could be, nothing or no one paid attention to her as far as she could tell. But she knew Ferenci was probably watching her. The bomb in the car was for when she got in. When the uniforms left without her, they ceased to be of any use to a man like Ferenci, so he disposed of them.

Where was Elmore? Where was Drake? Could Ferenci

already have Drake?

She made it to the door of a restaurant called The Babur. A loud crack reverberated from across the street. People on the other sidewalk ducked as the restaurant window behind her shattered.

Gun.

That was enough to get her running, bad knee or not.

She ran hard for the corner, turned around it, and bumped into Parkman.

"What the hell is going on out here?" he asked.

"The car … it exploded … someone shot at me … Ferenci," Sarah managed to get out between breaths.

"What?" Spencer asked. "Slow down. What's going on?"

Sarah leaned on Parkman's arm, her leg pain flaring up. It struck her as odd at that moment that she would notice Parkman didn't have a toothpick in his mouth.

"What happened to your toothpick?"

Parkman frowned. He looked at Spencer. "Elmore is dead. We found his body. He was shot in each leg and a couple of times in the face."

Sarah breathed easier. She pushed off Parkman's arm, stood on her own, and stepped away. "Good. Sounds like Ferenci did something right." She turned to Spencer. "Two uniforms showed up when I stood waiting for you two in the alley. They escorted me at gunpoint to a car. If I hadn't escaped, I would've died in that car. It just exploded on Queen Street. It was Ferenci. I'm assuming he has Drake. They just shot at me around that corner." She pointed back to where she'd just come from, still trying to catch her breath.

Spencer got on his radio. "Lock down a two-block radius. Roadblock on each route leaving this area."

He ran away from them, pulling his weapon and heading for the corner. A moment later, he disappeared around the corner.

"You doing okay?" Parkman asked. "You're bleeding."

"Yeah, I'm good."

A gun went off, sounding like a firecracker. A woman screamed. It came from Queen Street, where Spencer had just run.

Parkman pulled his weapon and jogged to the corner to take a look with Sarah close behind. A number of people had gathered around the burning car. What caught their eye was the old man standing over Spencer, who now lay out on the sidewalk on his back. The old man aimed a gun at Spencer's forehead.

Parkman didn't call out. He didn't identify himself as a police officer. He just brought his gun up, aimed, and fired. It was a clean shot. The old man's head snapped sideways, and a spatter of blood sprayed out the other side. The old man fell hard as if he had been asleep on his feet.

Sarah took in the entire scene. She looked at all the witnesses, all the stopped cars. Mothers were covering their children's faces. Teenagers, their mouths agape. The huge man in a long overcoat across the street broke up the scene for her. He had a weapon, and he stared at them. As she watched, he lowered it and stuck it in the back of his pants.

"Parkman," she said as he came out of his shooter's stance. "That big guy over there has a gun, too."

Parkman snapped his attention to where Sarah pointed. "The guy in the navy blue overcoat? The one who just turned and started walking away?"

"Yeah, him. He jammed it in the back of his pants."

"On it," Parkman said and started across the street in pursuit.

Sarah leaned up against the wall and watched everything as best she could, looking for a threat. Police and an ambulance approached to attend to Spencer. She could check on him at any time, but if there was another shooter, she could be shot at any moment, so she kept watching the street.

After a full minute of standing in the early afternoon sun and scanning the entire area, she felt confident no one else posed a threat unless a shooter was hunched down in an obscure spot, in which case she couldn't do anything about it.

She needed to locate Drake.

She watched as Parkman caught up with the guy in the trench coat just over a block away. Maybe he'd know where Drake was. The guy raised his hands and got down on one knee. Parkman applied handcuffs, got the man standing again, and started toward Sarah.

The car the man had been standing beside when Sarah saw him moved. She shaded her eyes from the sun and looked again. Sure enough, the car moved ever so slightly. She pushed off the wall and walked across Queen Street, weaving through the slow-moving vehicles that skirted the burning car.

She neared the car. It was idling.

This was their getaway car. They wanted to shoot me and drive away.

The front door wasn't locked. She opened it and saw the keys in the ignition.

The car moved and shook a little again, this time accompanied by a moan.

The trunk.

She pushed the automatic release button by the bottom edge of the driver's seat and walked back to the trunk.

The lid lifted without resistance. A crowbar flew out at her. She dodged left, the steel bar missing her face by less than an inch.

"Drake!" She was so happy to see him.

"Sarah? Oh, shit, I'm sorry. I had no idea."

She grabbed his good wrist and helped him out.

"No problem … just don't throw shit at me. Pisses me off."

"No problem. I didn't know. Sorry."

The bullet wound in his leg had bled out more. His jeans were matted in blood, and his face was pale.

"Are you okay? How are you feeling?" she asked.

"Yeah. I'm good. They're gone, and you're here, so yeah, I'm good. I just hate getting shot. Any chance we can stop having me get shot?"

"We have to get you to that ambulance. Those paramedics can help—"

"No," he cut her off. "Just get me out of here. Take me to the Trillium Health Center. It's on the West Mall. I'll show you. I just need to get out of here. Who knows who'll pop up next with a gun and a desire to murder us?"

She looked at him for a second longer and then nodded. "You got it. Get in."

Sarah helped him to the passenger side, and after he was settled in, she ran around to the driver's side of Ferenci's car, jumped in, and edged out into traffic.

Drake grabbed a blanket from the back seat, covered his blood-covered jeans, then lay his head back and closed his eyes.

"You know, Sarah," he said. "You've saved my life twice now. That means I'm yours forever. I owe you my life. I know this may sound corny, but seriously, I'd be dead without you. I don't have a death wish, but I know now that I will die in your place if it ever comes down to it."

Sarah didn't respond. She couldn't. It was the nicest thing anyone had ever said to her before. No one had ever said they would die for her, and she believed him.

The traffic slowed. Up ahead, four police cruisers blocked the road, leaving a narrow path where vehicles were allowed to go through once they were cleared.

There were two cars left, and then an officer would ask questions neither one could answer. She didn't know where the papers were. For all she knew, Ferenci could've stolen the car, and now she was driving it after stealing it from him.

Fuck. Now what?

"Don't panic," she said. "We'll get through this. Follow my lead. And remember, we've done nothing wrong. I'm just getting us out of the area before someone picks us off."

A Toronto police officer walked up to her window and asked her to roll it down.

"Evening, Officer," Sarah said, a wide, innocent smile creasing her face. "What seems to be the trouble?"

"Where are you two headed?" he asked as he looked in at Drake.

"To our uncle's place for dinner."

"Really? Were you anywhere near the explosion on Queen Street?"

"There was an explosion on Queen Street? Wow … what blew up?" Sarah asked in her dumb-blond voice. She wondered if she poured it on too thick as her voice squeaked with the higher pitch.

The officer eyed her too long. He looked in at Drake again. "You okay over there? You look a little pale."

Drake nodded. "Yeah, just seriously hungry, and her uncle cooks up a mean lasagna."

The cop looked at Sarah and pointed at Drake. "He your boyfriend?"

Sarah glanced at Drake and said, "Yes."

What the fuck? Too soon. It came out too quickly. Shit, what will Drake think?

"Okay." The officer stood to his full height and adjusted his belt, staring at Sarah with what she thought was anger.

He's going to fucking call us on our bullshit.

"A moment ago, you said our uncle, and then your boyfriend said your uncle. So which is it, because I'm starting to wonder about you two?"

Now what?

Another cop walked up behind the one talking to them. "Everything okay here, Officer Jones?"

He turned around, "Yeah, I got this. Just give me another second."

"Okay, I'm going to make you pull over there so I can grill you and take you downtown and make things very difficult for as long as I can because I'm an asshole like that and because I think you're lying to me. But if you're both just running away from mommy and you're wasting my time by lying to me, then I need you out of my face. So here's how it's going to go." He bent and placed his forearm along the door getting his face low enough to look in at Drake, too. "Tell me your uncle's name at the same time at the count of three. If you can do that, I'll assume the story isn't made up, and you're on the level. Deal?"

Sarah nodded, gritting her teeth.

He lifted his sleeve to look at his watch. "One. Two. Three."

Please, say the same one as me.

"Uncle Rod," they both said in perfect harmony.

The officer stood to his full height and knocked on the roof of their car to motion them through.

Sarah drove between the two cruisers and onto the open road. They looked at each other and started breathing again.

They'd made it. Her heart beat in anticipation of what her life was about to become. They'd made it. They were out. But now she seemed even more afraid because of the man in the seat beside her. He could hurt her more than the bullets, bruises, and fights she'd endured over the last five years.

Drake had a weapon that cut her on the inside.

If they began a relationship, she'd voluntarily walk into it and willingly make herself a target. That was something altogether foreign to her. She had no idea what to do.

Her hands shook on the wheel of Ferenci's car. She wondered if Drake would notice. Her face felt flush.

What the hell is wrong with me? Do I or don't I? Would I or won't I?

But she had no choice now.

"That was close," Drake said.

"Very," Sarah said.

She focused on her driving as the afternoon sun beat down on the windshield.

Chapter 37

ONE MONTH LATER …

The waiter directed them to a quiet table by an old train car near the center of the restaurant. Sarah gawked at the sight of the train car, having come to love the uniqueness of Toronto.

Sarah pulled out her own chair and sat. It had been a month since Ferenci had tried to kill Drake at the baseball game. At that time, she had set a few rules down for the romantic Drake. One of those had been that she would pull out all her own chairs. Wooing was nice, even pleasant at times, but she needed to go slow as a relationship violated her independence to the core. She told him she was willing to try, but it had to be friends first—spend time together—get to know one another. Then work from there.

Every event wasn't a date, and every date wasn't an invitation or an expectation.

Drake had agreed without pause.

He sat across from her and smiled. "I just can't believe

it," he said. "It's finally over. Ferenci is dead. His hired muscle is in jail, and Elmore is dead. I don't know how we did it, but we're the ones walking away." He looked into her eyes. "Sometimes, I still can't believe it. I never thought I would be happy that another human being was dead, but some people don't deserve life."

"They might want to think about banning police scanners, too. I mean, Ferenci heard the call for all officers to respond to Elmore's studio and beat the cops there by five full minutes. Because of that scanner, you could have been killed before anyone got there."

Drake picked up the menu. "I know. I shudder when I think about it. When Ferenci opened Elmore's trunk, I thought he'd shoot me on the spot. Using those fake cops to get to you almost worked."

Sarah looked at the name on the menu. "The Old Spaghetti Factory. What made you pick this place for dinner? Is it good?"

"Sure. It's one of the best in Toronto. Anyone who has been in this city for more than a decade has come here at least once." Drake dropped his menu back to the table. "Sarah, what do you think of Toronto so far?"

Sarah smiled and set her menu down, too. "It's been amazing. I've never been this free. I'm finally completely free. No one is stalking me or hunting me down. After what Rod did for me, I'm eternally grateful."

She picked her menu up again and browsed the wine list while she thought about Rod. He'd gotten out of the hospital two weeks ago and headed back to the States alone, ready to retire from the Sophia Project. Sarah could have run from Elmore's basement and left him to die. Instead, she had brought help in time to save his life. For that, he'd told her he would take her file and report it as unfounded. Sarah Roberts had no special abilities, he would say. As far as he was concerned, his agency would have no further interest in her. She could be free to do whatever she wanted without worrying about their group anymore. Although she remembered his one caution: keep under the radar.

The waiter set fresh bread on their table. Sarah breathed in deeply as the smell wafted up. She ordered an Australian red, and Drake chose a domestic beer.

She admired his ability to ignore his wounds. He'd healed quickly with an attitude that any physiologist would love. He repeatedly said his muscles would learn. Even though they ached and he limped, he refused to use any crutch. He'd walk on the bad leg until it learned to right itself. He sounded a little foolish to her at first, but he was coming along great, barely limping.

Parkman had flown back to his job as his leave of absence had ended. She missed him but knew they'd see each other again soon. She wanted to take Drake to the States to meet Esmerelda and her daughter, Denise. She couldn't take Drake all that way and not meet Dolan, too. Whether she let Drake meet her parents or not was something she'd have to consider. How serious were they, or how serious were they going to be?

"Tell me more about Vivian. When was the last time she got in touch?"

Sarah adjusted herself in her chair. "I miss hearing from her. She sent me a message a week ago apologizing for not helping more with Elmore more. She had decided to stop with the messages as Armond had been dealt with, and so had

Ferenci. She felt she had put me in harm's way too often. It's all over, she claimed. I have tried to talk to her numerous times but still haven't gotten a reply."

"Tell me about Esmerelda and Dolan," Drake said.

The waiter showed up with their drinks. Sarah sniffed her wine, spun it in the glass, and then sipped. After another sip, she set it down.

"She's a lovely woman. She lives with her daughter now. You'll meet them one day."

"How do you know her and Dolan?"

"Long story. Order me another glass of wine, and I'll tell you all about it. Our trip to the States will be great." She took another sip. "It's been a long time since I've felt this free."

Sarah leaned to look past Drake toward a commotion at the front of the restaurant. He turned in his chair.

A group of men in business suits argued with their waiter. Sarah watched as one of the men pushed the waiter aside and stepped farther into the restaurant.

Her stomach lurched. She hadn't been without trouble for this long and wondered for weeks if trouble would find her again. The man looked ex-military with his buzz-cut hair and hard, chiseled features. The men behind him watched his every move and waited for an order.

She picked up her wine glass and sipped from it.

"That's fuckin' rude," Drake said as he turned back in his seat.

Drake grabbed the bread and broke a piece off.

The men spread into the restaurant in a search-grid formation. It was evident to Sarah that they were looking for someone.

As the leader looked at the face of a girl six tables over,

Sarah detected the butt of a weapon protruding through the fabric of the man's jacket.

"Drake, they're packing. This may not be cool. Be ready."

He stopped buttering his bread and stared at her. "You're kidding, right? Who could it be? We were cleared on everything. Spencer backed us up along with Rod on the entire story. We were the victims—"

"Shhh, they're coming our way."

The leader stepped behind Drake and stared at Sarah. Then he whistled with his fingers like he was playing Frisbee in a park with no regard for being in a classy restaurant. All of his men turned and started toward them.

"Sarah Roberts?"

She took another sip of her wine and set the glass down, her stomach in knots.

What now?

"That depends," she said.

The man raised his eyebrows. "On what?" he asked.

"Who you are." She wrapped her hand around the butter knife on her side of the table. "I can be Sarah Roberts for the right price, but I can also be Maggie May. Does that sound right, Mr. Stewart?"

"Your reference to Rod is spot on. How could you tell we were agency men?" He waited for her to respond. "My name is Hank Frommer. I'm the new main man for the Sophia Project now that Rod has retired."

"Never heard of it," Sarah said as she took a larger sip of wine.

Shit, fuck!

The men circled the table. It couldn't be. Rod had said

she was covered. It would never come back to haunt her unless she became too public. Vivian had stopped sending her messages. She'd gone on no expeditions of any kind in Toronto.

"You'll have to come with us. There's been a problem. We need to clear it up."

"I'm not going anywhere with you." Then she thought for a second and asked, "What kind of problem?"

"I don't think you understand. Rod Howley filed a report clearing you of all suspicion of any psychic ability. I know he lied. You have no choice but to come with me. Stand up and come willingly. I want this to be a pleasant experience for all of us. Otherwise, we will take you by force." He swept his arms out at his men like he was displaying a prize on the Price Is Right. "I know you're unarmed except for that butter knife. If you decide to use that knife, I will have you incarcerated for many years for assault on a Federal Officer. That will give us plenty of time to get to know one another." He stepped closer and put his hand out. "Stand up now. You are coming with us as you are officially the property of the United States of America."

Sarah felt everyone in the restaurant watching the action unfold. Their waiter stood fifteen feet behind Hank. The tension around them seemed to increase by the second as everyone waited to see what Sarah would do.

Drake winked at her.

It broke her concentration. In his wink, she read, *I got this.*

She nodded ever so slightly and let go of the butter knife. She moved her chair back and grabbed her wine for one more sip. Then she stood and scanned the faces of the men surrounding her.

She addressed Drake. "I'm sorry our dinner was so rudely interrupted. I recommend we reschedule."

Drake pushed his chair out and stood with his beer in his hand. Hank's men closed in on Drake as a warning.

"It's okay, dear. How about tomorrow? We'll find a location where these men can't harass us. Sound good?"

"Lovely. It's a date, then."

Drake spun on his heels, a beer bottle held high. In that second, Sarah tossed her wine in Hank's face. Drake's beer bottle broke on the first guy's face and cut into the faces of the two men beside him.

Sarah dodged Hank's grasp, grabbed the knife, and jammed it into the thigh of the man beside her. He shouted and dropped to the carpeted floor. She grabbed the top of her chair and swung it hard and fast at Hank, who at that same moment stepped toward her. The chair broke across his chest and jaw, and he staggered back.

Surprisingly, she bolted for the rear of the restaurant with Hank on her heels. She hit the kitchen door and kept running, knowing Hank would be close behind.

She ran into the dark Toronto night in the alley at the back of the restaurant.

Hank wouldn't fire on her to kill her.

She had no idea where she was going or what she'd do. Normally she'd find a bus or a train and escape Toronto, but because of Drake, she couldn't.

She had to go back and see what was happening to him, but she couldn't do that either. He'd be angry that they wasted their efforts at escape only for her to come back.

It was time to talk to Vivian. It was time to set things

right. Sarah's life needed a save now so she could have one. A happy one.

Vivian owed her. Vivian owed her Drake. She owed her peace, but most of all, Vivian needed to save Sarah's life, as Sarah had made things right for Vivian.

And she knew exactly how to get Vivian to talk.

Sarah turned around and started back toward the restaurant and Hank Frommer.

It was time to stop the insanity, and she intended to show the American government everything she was.

How powerful she could be.

It was time for the world to see Sarah Roberts and for Sarah Roberts to see the world.

She only hoped she was making the right decision.

Her hand went numb. Before passing out in the street, Sarah cried out, "Vivian?"

Chapter 38

Sarah opened her eyes. She jumped to her feet and looked up and down the street. No cars approached.

"What just happened to you? Are you okay?" a man asked from her right.

She spun in that direction and saw Hank. He held a weapon aimed at the ground.

"I asked, what just happened to you?"

"If this is what it takes," Sarah whispered under her breath. "Then let's do this. But Vivian, don't let me down here. I need you."

"Who are you talking to?" Hank asked.

Sarah started toward him. As she drew closer, he raised his weapon.

"Be careful, Sarah," he warned. "No more hero stuff. My jaw still aches, but my patience is suffering."

She stopped four feet in front of him and offered her wrists. "If you're worried, then cuff me."

He looked at her proffered arms and then back at her.

"Why?"

"Why what?"

"Why fight and then come willingly?"

"Because you'll never go away. If you people don't understand me, I'll give you a chance to, and then, maybe, you'll go away and leave me alone."

"You serious?" Hank lowered his weapon again.

Sarah nodded.

"Rod told me to be careful, that you never bluff. I was instructed to take you at your word, even if I find it dangerous." He started walking and said over his shoulder, "Follow me."

Sarah kept close. "What's going to happen to Drake?"

"Nothing. We aren't concerned about filing petty charges when a man wants to protect his woman. My men are prepared for violence. Drake got the better of us."

"Some of your men were really hurt back there," Sarah said, her tone one of disbelief.

"How secret do you think my organization would be if we legally pursued infractions on my men? Sitting in court, trying to explain our presence there and what caused Drake, or you, to attack us. We run things behind a veil, and that means everything."

Hank approached a black H2 Hummer. A driver hopped out and opened the back door. Hank motioned for Sarah to get in.

She turned to look at the restaurant.

Sorry, Drake. I promise we'll have dinner again soon.

The back seat of the Hummer was a virtual prison. The doors were thick, and bars separated the front from the back. The driver must have driven a Hummer since he was a child in how he handled the wheel.

At first, she couldn't tell where they were headed but figured the airport soon enough. After fifteen minutes, Sarah recognized the fence surrounding the airport. The driver pulled up to a guarded entrance and was waved through. Seconds later, the driver stopped beside a Lear jet.

"This is it," Hank said. He turned in his seat to address Sarah. "Are we going to have a problem?"

"No."

"Good. Let's go."

The door beside her clicked. She got out and walked up the steps into the airplane.

After taking a seat halfway down, she asked, "Where are we flying to?"

Hank had stepped in behind her and was talking to the pilots. He stopped talking and turned to her. "To a unique facility where we will talk. That's it. You tell me what you do and how you do it." He stepped closer and sat in a chair opposite hers. "I'll need a demonstration. Then we'll talk again. If what you do serves our aims, we will discuss the future. If it doesn't, I'll have these pilots fly you wherever you want to go, and you'll never hear from the Sophia Project again. Sound good to you?"

"I'm sure I want to get this over with more than you. Also, I'm confident that what I do will be of no use to you."

"How so?"

"Because my sister only gives me details that fit a specific situation. Like the news anchorwoman five years ago. I was told to bring a hammer and wait under the bridge. Once I saw the car accident, I did what any other human being would do. I ran for the woman drowning in her car and tried to get in. Because I had a hammer, I could break the window and save the woman. That's it. What I do will not solve wars or tell you where hidden nukes are. If this is a way to add me to the payroll of the war machine, you have the wrong girl. Trust me."

Hank seemed to hear her. He appeared to digest what she'd said as he formulated a response.

The engines revved, and the plane advanced forward. Sarah closed her eyes and waited until they took off before she opened them again.

"You're missing one thing," he said.

"What's that?"

"You said Vivian gives you these messages, right?"

Sarah nodded.

"Would it be safe to assume that even though what you do is dangerous, Vivian would never knowingly send you into a situation where you would outright die? Evidently, since you're sitting here before me, living, breathing, I already know the answer to that question."

"Where are you going with this?"

"Vivian loves you. She adores you."

"Agreed. Your point?"

"She would never let anything happen to you."

"You've stated that. Stop going in circles."

"Meaning, I could threaten to harm you or even harm you on purpose, and Vivian would start producing." He turned in his seat to talk face-to-face with her. "Do you see where I'm going with this? I could force her hand. I could make her talk through you and tell me what I want to know once I have you hooked up to an electric chair where, depending on the voltage, I could cause you great harm or a 5.2 on the Richter Scale over ten years ago, and no one in the building felt a thing. You have nothing to worry about."

"Why is it empty?" Sarah asked.

"They moved the headquarters to Winnipeg. Since late 2006, the complex has remained empty. The power cavern heats and ventilates the complex to avoid decay. My organization borrows it from time to time. The Americans paid over half to have this thing built, and many were brought up to work and train here for dozens of years. It's almost our property, so I use it as often as I need."

"Lucky you."

They made it to an elevator. Hank swiped a card. The men following them created a semicircle around Sarah and maintained a five-foot distance.

"No, lucky you."

"Why me?" she asked. "What's this big rock got to do with me?"

"I want to see if Vivian will come to you sixty stories down. I want to see how psychic you are. And what better place to do it but where you have no hope of escape."

She watched his chiseled face and built body under the suit jacket and wondered how often he worked out to create such a look.

"What makes you think I can't just walk away right now?"

"These friends of mine wouldn't allow that."

The elevator door opened. Sarah looked inside and, for the first time, realized that she may not be coming back up.

She stepped on and considered trying to get away but then dismissed the idea as soon as it developed. She had come here for a reason. Witnesses saw Hank go for her.

Drake and Parkman would be relentless if she didn't show up in a few days. Somehow, someway, Sarah would be coming up the elevator again.

The doors closed. She couldn't help but feel trapped.

"Oh, and the other reason there will be no escape is we have special doors on the facility downstairs."

"Special doors?"

"As an added security measure and the possibility of a nuclear strike, the builders added three nineteen-ton steel vault-type doors to the downstairs entrance. Nothing gets through them. Not even you, Sarah, not even you."

"You know what you remind me of?"

Hank turned to face her. He smiled. "Okay, I'll bite. What?"

"A priest writing a sermon on humility and then filing it away to be pulled out at a special event where you could impress a lot of people."

He frowned and looked at the men standing at his sides. "What? A priest?"

"Never mind."

The elevator stopped, and the doors opened to a huge corridor.

They stepped out as a group. The men guided Sarah to a room. She entered it, and they closed the door behind her.

Without another word, Hank and his men left her alone to wait until they decided the waiting would end.

I am so sick and tired of being held against my will. This is going to be the last time. Never again.

She examined every corner of the empty room. On the floor in the middle sat a thick pad of lined paper and three pens. Other than that, the square room was empty.

Sarah walked over to the pad, grabbed a pen, and lay down on the floor. A moment later, she was unconscious.

When she woke, the pad was littered with words scrawled out in her handwriting.

Sarah got up and crawled to the wall, where she leaned her back against it. After all the years together, her sister had never abandoned her.

The first page read:

Sarah. I'm committed to getting you out of there. Hank's wife. In six days, she will be killed at the Eaton Center in downtown Toronto. But you can't tell Hank yet.

Sarah flipped the page and continued reading.

I will send you five days of accidents, and together we'll save lives. You will be able to prove to Hank that you only do good things. When he wants a message of anything specific, you will come up empty. It'll frustrate him, but he'll believe in you by then. He will have too much proof. Then you tell him about his wife and explain that only you can attend to the mugging. That will be the deal.

Sarah flipped to the next page.

Rod Howley will learn of your incarceration in two days. He will be the one who devises the plan against Hank's wife to get you out. He won't kill her. He is only threatening her. The morning of the mugging, Rod Howley will call Hank and order your release. Hank will already know about the mugging because of you. He will put it all together. If he doesn't bring you, he loses his wife. He will also learn that you weren't bluffing and understand the gravity of the situation. He will feel you're more of an ally than Rod. Hank's downfall will be putting his trust in you.

Sarah flipped to the last page.

Hank has already killed seven others down here that didn't prove to be psychic. At least not in the way he needed them to be. Hank is upstairs, preparing the cyanide that will kill. There's nothing that can stop him. If you and Rod don't successfully get you out of this underground complex, you will be murdered in seven days by Hank Frommer, and he will file you as a missing person.

I'm sorry, Sarah.

If this doesn't work, you have seven days left to live.

About Jonas Saul

Jonas Saul is the bestselling author of the Sarah Roberts Series—more than two million sold!—and has written and published over sixty thrillers. After acquiring an agent, he signed several deals in Los Angeles, with MadRiver Pictures optioning his Sarah Roberts Series—over forty books!—(currently in development).

Jonas has often outranked Stephen King and Dean

Koontz on Amazon over the past decade. He's regularly invited to be a guest speaker, teacher, or workshop presenter at international writing conferences and film festivals worldwide. He hosts an annual writer's retreat in Greece, where he currently lives. He focuses his teaching on how to get tension and emotion in every scene, on every page, how he made it as a creator/writer, the path to success in this business, and the pitfalls to avoid. He also hosts a reading retreat in Greece with guest authors, yoga retreats, and hiking retreats. Visit the Imagine Greece Retreats website at www.imaginegreeceretreats.com, or email him directly to discuss an opportunity to join one of the retreats at jonas@imaginegreeceretreats.com.

Jonas is also a professional freelance editor. He works for several publishers and does private editing for clients, with many testimonials on his website at www.imaginepress.org, which details each author's response to Jonas's editing skills. Email Jonas directly for an editing quote at editor@imaginepress.org.

To book Jonas for a speaking engagement at a writer's conference/festival, to have him on your jury at a film festival, or even to say hello, email Jonas directly at jonassaul@icloud.com.

For updates on releases, hit the "Follow" button on Amazon or Bookbub, and join Jonas on Facebook, where he's most active.

Contact Jonas Saul

Linktree: Find me here

Email: jonassaul@icloud.com

www.ingramcontent.com/pod-product-compliance
Lightning Source LLC
Chambersburg PA
CBHW061549210726
48287CB00006B/2123